The Venus Fly-Trap

THE VENUS
FLY-TRAP

John Wainwright

ST. MARTIN'S PRESS
NEW YORK

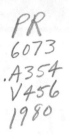

PR
6073
.A354
V456
1980

All rights reserved. For information, write:
St. Martin's Press, Inc., 175 Fifth Avenue, New York, N.Y. 10010
Manufactured in the United States of America
Library of Congress Catalog Card Number: 79–22757

Printed in the United States of America

Library of Congress Cataloging in Publication Data

Wainwright, John William, 1921–
   The Venus Fly-Trap.

   I. Title.
PZ4.W1418Ve   1980   [PR6073.A354]   823'.9'14
ISBN 0–312–83870–0   79–22757

Steps. They lead up, they lead down. They lead to glory; equally they lead to infamy. Take the number 'thirteen'. An unlucky number . . . and why? Because time was when that was the required number of steps leading up to the platform; to the block and the axe and the headsman. Later to the public hangman. Always thirteen, which makes the modern bingo-caller's 'unlucky for some' sound a trifle macabre.

But, what the hell, he doesn't know. All he's interested in is dancing ping-pong balls. He is far too busy to worry about steps.

Nevertheless, steps . . .

Few would argue that the handful of broad, shallow steps leading into and out of the arcade-like entrance to the Central Criminal Court have been ascended – and descended – by some of the biggest scoundrels ever to disgrace the not-too-honourable name of mankind. The villains. The frighteners. The swindlers. The fraudsters. The whoremasters. The hoodlums. Name the crime – name the infamy – and one or more of its representatives have swaggered up or down those steps.

Nor, be it understood, merely the evil.

Forensic giants of English legal history have used those steps. Sombrely dressed men and women from the Inns of Court; from the Temple, from Gray's, from Lincoln's. Barristers, solicitors, clerks and, in the old days, serjeants-at-law. Forensic scientists and police informants. Witnesses and complainants. And, of course, sightseers and ordinary people who wish to set foot within the world's greatest temple of justice . . . the Old Bailey.

And on this particular Wednesday afternoon two men walked side by side from the shadows of the entrance hall, down those steps and into the November daylight of the street.

5

Throughout their exit they did not speak. More than that. A careful watcher might have thought they tiptoed down that short flight of steps. As if a little afraid. As if not yet able to fully believe their good fortune; as if not yet able to fully appreciate the near-infallibility of British justice.

In age the two men were a generation apart. They were father and son; Sidney and Edward Palmer.

The elder man, Sidney Palmer, had the outward appearance of a novelist's notion of the average butler; ramrod-backed, but stocky and running to fat; bowler-hatted and wearing a dark grey overcoat over a navy blue suit, white shirt and slate-grey tie. He gave the impression of 'respectability' personified. Of quiet dignity. Of natural honesty.

And yet the eyes had a haunted, frightened look. A look associated with suffering. A puzzled look, as if the world – *his* world – had done something well beyond his own limited comprehension.

Edward (Eddie) Palmer on the other hand was of the present day. Slim and with hair too long to be other than unruly in the November breeze. He wore neither mac nor overcoat and his flared trousers, wine-coloured jacket, pale yellow shirt and dark red bow-tie paid scant homage to the nip of oncoming winter.

On him there was an expression of relief. Relief amounting to sheer joy. Relief which, it seemed, might cause him to burst into unrestrained laughter at any moment.

And yet, both men had one thing in common. The facial pallor, the deepened eye-sockets and the lines of recent worry.

Sidney Palmer seemed about to stumble as he reached the bottom of the steps, and Eddie cupped a hand under his father's left elbow to steady him.

When they reached the pavement, Eddie said, 'Okay, pop.'

Sidney Palmer nodded and tried to smile reassurance.

'Hang on, pop. I'll get transport.'

Eddie gave his father's arm an encouraging pat, then stepped to the kerb edge and signalled a passing taxi. As he climbed into the rear of the taxi Sidney's legs trembled slightly. Eddie gave the driver an address in Poplar, then joined his father.

Neither of them spoke for some time.

Their silence held until the taxi reached the Whitechapel area. Sidney rode with his head tilted back and the nape of his neck resting against the cool material of the upholstery. Eddie selected a cigarette from a slim-line case, lighted it, then smoked meditatively.

Almost apologetically Eddie murmured, 'It had me worried.'

Still staring at the roof of the taxi Sidney said, 'I'm glad it's over.'

'Yeah.' Eddie frowned – scowled at the glowing end of the cigarette – then said, 'Y'know, you didn't seem to give a damn. All the way through. I've watched you. Just standing there. Not giving a damn.'

'I expected prison.'

'Y'mean . . .'

'It's over, Eddie.' Sidney Palmer straightened his head. His flickered smile was sad. Nostalgic. 'It won't come back. None of it. The good. The bad. None of it will ever come back.'

There was more silence. The taxi threaded its way east, through the traffic and into Stepney. Eddie smoked his cigarette and occasionally glanced at the drawn face of his father. There was love, love almost amounting to worship, in his eyes.

He hesitated then said, 'It's over, pop.'

'I know.'

'It's all over.'

'Thank God,' sighed Sidney Palmer.

'Now . . .' The hesitation of a different nature. Awkward. Anxious. Eddie said. 'Now, you can tell us.'

'Tell you?'

'Tell *me* at least.'

'Whether your father's a murderer or not?' The timid, flickering smile touched the lips again.

Very softly Eddie said, 'It really doesn't matter a damn.'

7

'No?'

'Not to me. Either way. I'll not tell ma. I know how it was. Exactly how it was.'

'Yes.' Sidney Palmer sighed again. 'That's one consolation. We both know how it was.'

Eddie waited for an answer to his question, but none came. Sidney Palmer moved his head to stare at the passing world as the taxi sped along Commercial Road, past the Regent's Canal Dock area and entered Limehouse.

Without looking round he said, 'How's your mother taken it all?'

'Y'know . . .' Eddie moved the hand holding the cigarette. It was a vague meaningless gesture.

'No. I don't know. Otherwise I wouldn't have asked.'

Eddie said, 'She wanted to come to court. Today, especially. I wouldn't let her.'

'Wise,' murmured Sidney.

'Yeah. I thought so.'

Sidney Palmer didn't reply.

Eddie went on, 'What with Daphne and everything.'

'Poor Daphne.' It was little more than a breath.

'Yeah.'

Sidney Palmer said, 'You have plenty of time to think in prison, Eddie. All the time in the world. Too much time.'

'Yeah, I suppose.'

As if repeating a well-learned litany, Sidney Palmer muttered, 'He probably deserved it. He probably deserved to die.'

Eddie growled, 'Amen to that.'

Eddie dabbed out his cigarette into one of the ashtrays as the taxi turned right, then left, into Poplar High Street.

He said, 'That damn gun.'

'I know.' Sidney Palmer continued to watch from the window of the taxi.

'So bloody stupid.'

'Guns are always trouble,' sighed Sidney Palmer.

'That for a fact. But, y'know . . .'

'Eddie.' Sidney Palmer turned his head and looked at his

son's face. 'Don't tell your mother, but I never thought I'd see these streets again. Don't tell her, but I was . . . ready.'

Eddie stretched an arm and placed it on his father's knee as he said. 'C'mon, pop. *You* didn't shoot him.'

'The police still think I did.'

'No.' Eddie shook his head.

'To them "Not Guilty" doesn't necessarily mean innocent.'

'Pop!'

'I had a good barrister.'

'The hell, pop, you were innocent.'

'I had a good barrister,' repeated Sidney Palmer. 'That's why I'm here. A good barrister and a sympathetic jury.'

The taxi braked to a halt. Eddie opened the nearside door, stepped on to the pavement, grinned and said, 'Stop worrying, pop. This is it. Get ready for the "Welcome home" routine.'

Tuesday, June 13th

Strictly speaking it was indeed Tuesday, June 13th, but head waiters employed by London night clubs tend to add the small hours on to the previous day, therefore, as far as Sidney Palmer was concerned, it was still Monday, June 12th. A Monday similar to most other Mondays; a Monday of aching bones and tired feet; a Monday in which, as always, he had been held directly responsible for all the minor mishaps which had occurred in the dining-cum-concert-room of *The Venus Fly-Trap*.

In the bedroom of his home, Sidney Palmer sat on a chair, eased off his shoes and began to massage his stockinged toes. Freda, his wife, was already in bed; had been in bed since ten o'clock the previous evening. It was a nightly ritual. The sort of ritual indulged in without conscious thought by long-married couples.

Freda had gone to bed at what she would have called 'a respectable hour'. Sidney Palmer had had a snack at *The Venus Fly-Trap* after the last customer had left. Then the wine waiter, who lived at Canning Town, had given him a lift home in the small hours. His key in the lock had awakened his wife and, for perhaps thirty minutes, while he undressed and washed prior to bed, Sidney Palmer and his wife talked.

Again it was almost ritualistic. The questions. The expected answers. They were all part of their life's weave; ordinary, unexciting, but vital. A portion of the day which over the years had become necessary before either could settle and sleep until morning.

'A hard day?' she asked.

'So-so.'

He stood up from the chair, unknotted his tie and placed it carefully over the back of the chair.

She said, 'I think Mr Hodge should employ more waiters.'

10

'There's enough.' Sidney Palmer stifled a yawn. 'It's a good place. Popular. We all have to work, that's all.'

'You'll never criticise him.' There was petulance in her tone.

'Why should I?'

He slipped the braces from his shoulders, unzipped his fly and removed his trousers. He emptied the pockets of keys, small change and a handkerchief, then folded the trousers carefully before placing them across the seat of the chair.

He said, 'There are worse bosses.'

There was a silence during which he removed his shirt and, with equal care, folded it neatly and placed it on the trousers.

Almost tentatively she asked, 'Was *she* there?'

'Daphne?'

'Was she there?' she repeated, but this time without the emphasis on the second word.

'Don't.' His reprimand was gentle. 'Daphne's our daughter. She has a name.'

'Oh, yes. her kind have a name.'

'Don't call her "she". Don't call her "her" or "her kind". She's our daughter.'

The mild vehemence was still there when she said, 'I wonder if *she* remembers that sometimes?'

'She's only a child, Freda.'

'Nineteen. Closing twenty. She isn't a child any more.'

'My child. Always will be.'

He left the bedroom for the adjoining bathroom. He began to clean his teeth.

His wife called, '*Was* she there tonight?'

'Yes.'

'All right,' she called. 'She's your child, that's what you say. Stop her.'

He rinsed out his mouth, then turned off the taps of the washbasin, before he said, 'How? How can I?'

'You're the head waiter. You can . . .'

'That's all. I work there, that's all.'

She waited until he'd washed and returned to the bedroom before saying, 'Hodge could . . .'

'Mr Hodge *could,*' he sighed. 'That doesn't mean he will.'

'Ask him.'

'Look, why should Mr Hodge concern himself with *our* . . . ?'

'Ask him,' she repeated.

'And then she'll go somewhere else.'

His wife said, 'What you mean is you can't control your own daughter.'

Sidney Palmer took his pyjamas from under his pillow and, as he stripped off his underpants and threaded his legs into the pyjamas, he said, 'If you say so.'

'That's a fine admission to make, isn't it?'

'Pet.' Long-sufferance was in his tone. 'Daphne's important, of course she is. But she's too old to spank. But my job's important, too. I have to balance the two. These people – these people she knocks about with – they have money. They spend. Mr Hodge wants them to spend. Booze. Meals. Gambling. That's his living. It's *my* living, too, come to that. If I upset that crowd, I could be on the street.'

'But . . .'

'But I'll ask him.' Sidney Palmer climbed into bed. 'I know what his answer will be, but I'll ask him.'

He reached up to the lazy-switch and turned off the light.

His wife said, 'How long will Eddie be?'

'I don't know. Maybe another hour . . . thereabouts. He was going to put the band through some new arrangement or other.'

Eddie Palmer fingered the valves on his trumpet, frowned at the tiny group of musicians with whom he worked and said, 'There's something not there. It's not smoochy enough.'

From the piano Paul said. 'Could be we're tired.'

'Yeah, could be we're tired,' agreed Eddie. 'Could be we're also pros. And *Lazy River* shouldn't plough us. Not even if we're asleep upright. It's a good new arrangement.' He spoke directly to the pianist. 'Try it on the organ, Paul. More basement. Nice, thick background chords. Sustained, eh? Something we can build on.'

12

The man called Paul turned on the swivelled-stool from the piano keyboard to the keyboard of the electronic organ. He fingered some bass chords. Musical doodling, pending Eddie's lead-in beat.

Eddie said, 'Okay, the rest of you. *Lazy River* . . . so make it lazy. Lazy, not sleepy.'

Hodge, the proprietor of *The Venus Fly-Trap,* walked briskly between the empty tables and stopped at the edge of the tiny stage. He was a stocky man, broad-shouldered but with a layer of fat where there had once been hard muscle. Nevertheless, and from outward appearances, a man not to be lightly argued with. Despite the hour, and the loosened tie, he still looked smart and alive; the dove-grey, double-breasted suit sat on his frame well . . . a frame it had been hand-made for.

He said, 'Call it a day, Eddie.'

Eddie Palmer lowered his trumpet to his side, frowned, then said, 'I'd like about half an hour, boss. Just to get this new arrangement under way.'

'Come in early tomorrow.'

'Okay.' Eddie shrugged. He turned to the musicians and added, 'That's it, boys. Make for the sheets. See you back here about noon. We'll iron the kinks out.'

The musicians grunted relieved agreement and began to case and close their various instruments.

Eddie Palmer drove the V.W. Beetle east through the near-deserted streets. He drove relaxed and easy. The old Beetle had sailed through her MoT test and, without the crush of daytime or evening traffic, she seemed almost to saunter her way home, guided by the light touch of one hand on the steering wheel.

Eddie Palmer was, if not completely happy, at least contented. This – the small, lonely hours – was his favourite o'clock. He was, he freely admitted, a lucky guy. Few luckier. His personal bag was jazz. Small combo jazz. Trad, with that little something necessary to lift it into mass popularity.

He had a shop-window, too. *The Venus Fly-Trap.* Hodge allowed him a fairly loose rein. At first it had been a couple of spots spaced throughout the evening. Now Eddie Palmer and *The Opus* provided the link between visiting performers; they held the stage for most of the time. Hodge, too, liked the old standards; the numbers the giants had flecked with gold; the foot-tappers guaranteed to make the customers forget their troubles, grin and spend big.

Okay, Hodge had the takings in mind, maybe. And why not? But – also maybe – Hodge had visions of making *The Fly-Trap* into one of the capital's top jazz spots.

Dreams? Okay, dreams. But this was the hour for dreams. This was the time on the clock when every jazzman in the world built his own castle of cards. Like now. Steering an old and slightly battered V.W, with more than eighty thousand on the clock and still going strong, through the short-cuts of the greatest city on earth.

That and building card-castles. Cosy. Contented. The world his for the taking. The cased horn, on the seat alongside him, the same instrument Bix, Louis and a group of 'greats' had used to blow their way to immortality.

Maybe Eddie Palmer . . . who could stamp out a dream at this hour?

A happy grin touched his lips. Then the grin disappeared as he remembered.

Jesus, why couldn't that sister of his get wise? Why couldn't she be only part-dumb? Why couldn't she smell the lice she kept company with? The brittle smart-arse crowd those two ran around with. For Christ's sake, she must *know.* The booze: holy cow, that party swilled it down like tomorrow was the end of the world. Yeah, and the other stuff. Pot. Grass. What the hell it was called these days. Okay, maybe she was. Maybe she wasn't. Who could tell these days? And if she did smoke the damn stuff, what of it? Harmless, that's what the wise people said. Less harmful than an ordinary cigarette. Okay, could be. But if she was on the soft stuff, what next? And there had to be 'next'. There always was.

So, okay, assuming she was on pot. If so, she wasn't alone.

14

Not by a Wembley football-final crowd. Some of the top showbiz crowd smoked grass.

Yeah. But . . .

Who could be sure? Maybe she was on snort-ups, too. Or even spiking for Christ's sake. The stupid little bitch. With that crowd anything . . . *anything*!

A strange mix of dreams and worries. A mental concoction, peculiar to a man who loved both his work and his sister. A concoction with a very low flash-point.

Soho.

Ask one Londoner and he will tell you that Soho is the district surrounding Soho Square. Ask another Londoner and he will tell you that Soho is bordered on the north by Oxford Street, on the east by Charing Cross Road, on the south by Shaftesbury Avenue and on the west by Wardour Street.

Ask a dozen Londoners and you will get a dozen different replies. The replies will include street names and a postal district. But the replies will mean little, because Soho is more than a built-up area. Soho is, primarily, a state of mind.

It is a place of strip-joints, blue-film cinemas and massage parlours. But it is also a place of well-attended churches, near-strait-laced respectability and well-above-average honour. A place of sin and saintliness; a Babel of great corruption and equally great honesty; the haunt and home of every emotion known to man. It is *the* melting-pot of races; just about the only spot on earth where skin pigmentation really doesn't matter a damn. It at once caters for every gradation of every religion, and every pornography, under the sun.

It is unique.

It is Soho.

Within its limits – whatever those limits are – can be found some of the best eating-houses and some of the best night-spots in London, which means in the world.

One such night-spot was *The Venus Fly-Trap*.

Like others of its kind it had to be known or it had to be

15

found. Its entrance was at the end of a not-too-well-lit cul-de-sac. Its entry was via a single door, below an almost shy neon sign and from there carpeted steps led below ground. But once there – once within the maze of cellarage upon which Soho stands – the extent and munificence of *The Venus Fly-Trap* came as a pleasant shock to any stranger.

The main room – the dining-cum-concert-room – seemed almost impossibly large; the tables were well spaced and, along one side of the room, the well-stocked bar was far more than a token gesture to those requiring booze. The room was, perhaps, low-ceilinged, but smooth-running extractor fans kept the air clean and sweet-smelling. Nor was the subdued lighting of 'working hours' meant to hide grime.

On this particular Tuesday afternoon the harsh glare of high-wattage bulbs gave ample light for the cleaners making ready for the seven-thirty opening and allowed the proprietor. Tommy Hodge, to check upon the sparkle of the glassware, cutlery and crockery, the starched whiteness of the table-linen.

On the miniature stage Eddie Palmer and his group of fellow-musicians, *The Opus,* were in concentrated rehearsal. Sidney Palmer – not yet in his uniform of white tie and tails – was moving from table to table, checking that everything was immaculate and, now and again, moving a knife or a fork into a more geometrical position.

There was no rush. The waiters – the cleaners – had done it all hundreds of times. The preparation; this setting of the scene for the seven-thirty rise of the curtain. Nothing new and yet . . .

As Hodge made for the doors leading to the kitchens Sidney Palmer hurried between the tables to intercept him.

Palmer said, 'Er – Mr Hodge.'

'Yeah?'

In that one-word question there was aggression. An aggression which went with the slacks and the sandals and the short-sleeved. open-necked towelling shirt; with the dark, unblinking eyes; with the thick-sinewed, hair-covered forearms.

Sidney Palmer knew he couldn't win. Nevertheless he tried.

He said, 'It's – er – it's about Daphne.'

'Your kid?'

'Yes.' Palmer nodded.

'A nice-looking kid.'

'Eh? Oh – er – yes, but I'm biased.'

'Take my word for it.'

'Thank you.' Palmer hesitated, then said, 'I – er – I promised my wife.'

'What?'

'That – that I'd ask you.'

'Ask me what?'

Sidney Palmer swallowed, then said, 'As a personal favour, Mr Hodge. Could you bar her . . . please?'

'Eh?' Hodge's eyes narrowed.

'From *The Venus Fly-Trap*. Refuse her admission.'

'What's wrong with *The Fly-Trap*?' growled Hodge.

'Nothing. Nothing at all. It's one of the . . .'

'Okay. One good reason why?'

'She's – she's in with the wrong crowd.'

'Customers, Palmer.'

'I – I . . .'

'They feed lettuce into the machine. And this is the machine.'

'Yes, sir. I know that. But . . .'

'Customers, don't forget that little point.'

'Look.' There was a hint of desperation in Palmer's pleading. 'Mr Hodge, if she was *your* daughter . . .'

'She's not my daughter. To me she's one more customer. She's there among the spenders. No deal, Palmer.' Hodge turned to walk away, changed his mind, and added. 'And – er – Palmer. Be wise. Don't push things.'

Hodge strode through the swing-doors leading to the kitchens.

And Sidney Palmer stood there. Crestfallen. Remembering. Reminding himself. The name of the ball game was 'money'. Loot. Lettuce, to use Hodge's expression. A few dozen ways

17

of saying the same thing. The only reason anybody did *anything*, or so it seemed.

You grafted your heart out, year after year. You turned day into night and night into day and you never complained. Okay, that's what you do. You think anybody takes *that* into consideration?

Old man, you're crazy. You're from another age. You're a hired help, old man; one more hired help. You're that and nothing more. And don't you ever forget it.

Eddie's voice said, 'It might never happen, pop.'

'What?'

Sidney Palmer jerked himself from the black mood and smiled a watery smile at his son. The members of *The Opus* had put aside their instruments and were lining the bar, ready for that single on-the-house drink before they ate, then changed into uniform and made ready for their opening number at eight o'clock.

Eddie said, 'Back to earth, pop. You were miles away.'

'Miles away,' admitted Palmer.

'Something wrong with Tommy?' Eddie jerked his head towards the doors through which Hodge had disappeared.

'He's all right.' Palmer's expression reflected pain and bitterness.

'Yeah, I'll bet.'

'Eddie, he's a good man.'

'That why you have a face like a wet weekend?'

'No, I mean it.' Again the sad half-smile. He's a good man. He's right. By his yardstick.'

'Yardsticks,' mused Eddie. 'They come in all lengths though, eh?'

Sidney Palmer took a deep breath. He pinched his nose above the bridge. It was a small gesture of weary defeat.

Eddie touched his father's arm and murmured, 'C'mon. Share it, pop.'

'Your mother asked,' sighed Palmer. 'A favour from Mr Hodge. To bar Daphne from *The Fly-Trap*.'

Eddie widened his eyes and said, 'That's my old man. Never ask for small favours. Think big.'

18

'I know. Your mother doesn't understand. She thinks I'm weak.'

'We're all weak, pop.' said Eddie gently. 'That's how people like us survive. In this jungle we're all either tigers or pussy cats. You? Me? We're strictly moggies. That way we don't lose our marbles. Daphne? Okay. Daphne: you should have slapped her fanny till she couldn't sit down for a week. You didn't. You're too nice a guy. A nice guy with a stupid bitch for a daughter, let's drink to *that*.'

Away from the atmosphere of the club proper Tommy Hodge was (to use Eddie's expression) much less 'tigerish'. He was no purring ball of fur, you understand; the hard core of autocracy, necessary for survival within his chosen field, was still there, but within the womb of the luxury flat above the club it was less aggressive, and his relaxation was as complete as it ever could be.

This was due in no small measure to his wife, Valda.

Valda, it really *was* her name.

A large-boned woman with flesh in all the right places. The immediate impression was of a female middleweight champion. That until you noticed her eyes. The eyes – and without the emphasis of make-up – were her dominant feature. They 'spoke' They conveyed every nuance of her mercurial nature.

And now as they both went about their business of preparing for the club's evening activity those eyes tended to flash a little.

Hodge had mentioned Sidney Palmer's request; merely mentioned it in small-talk. And Valda's reaction had startled him.

As she settled her figure more comfortably into the 'foundation garments' which aided her majestic appearance she snapped, 'So? One bird-brained little chick. We throw more profit than she brings into the food-bins every night.'

'Don't you believe it,' growled Hodge. 'That one attracts the spenders.'

'She's a teenage tart.'

'Okay – she's a teenage tart. She's not the first. She won't be the last. But she has expensive tastes and boy-friends to match.'

'And Palmer?' Valda flicked the dresses in the wardrobe, made her choice, then slid it from its hanger. 'He's no new kid we've just started. He's been here since God knows when. He deserves a break.'

'Forget it, honey. He's on the payroll.'

'So? He works his way. He's no passenger.'

She stepped into the dress and threaded her arms through the sleeves.

Hodge grinned at his own reflection in the dressing-table mirror as he adjusted his tie.

He said, 'When I need Hearts and Flowers, I'll hire some clown with a violin.'

'He's a nice guy,' insisted Valda.

'Palmer?'

'Palmer. He's a nice guy.'

'Yeah. We're all nice guys. Nice and nasty. Whichever pays.'

'He's nice,' insisted Valda.

'Okay. Who's arguing?'

'A little weak, maybe.'

'Fine, let him be weak on his own time.'

She backed towards Hodge, in order that he might zip up her dress.

She said, 'A small favour. That's all he's asking.'

Hodge zipped up the fastener as if the movement was the punctuation mark at the end of an unwanted paragraph.

He growled, 'A small favour. Honey, people end up on the breadline doing small favours.'

Not that *The Venus Fly-Trap* could be viewed as having any direct, or even indirect, connection with such wretched things as breadlines. The 'bread' which that establishment handled was of the green variety, carried around in billfolds. There was indeed a smooth, lush warmth about the luxury it offered; a smiling. well-oiled welcome which made it almost a pleasure to eat and drink like a prince . . . and pay a king's ransom for the privilege.

At eight o'clock (on the button) Eddie Palmer brought his trumpet to his lips as the curtains of the tiny stage swung aside and led with a glissando into the opening bars of *Opus One*.

Opus One; the big-band classic which will forever be linked with the name of Tommy Dorsey. And yet *The Opus* – because it was *called The Opus* – had caught it as a signature tune. Caught it and re-vamped it.

Including Eddie Palmer the combo was a seven-piece outfit. Standard, until you started permutating the various 'doublings'; the second, and sometimes third, instruments each player could handle. Eddie Palmer; trumpet and leader, doubling flugelhorn, cornet and valve-trombone. Paul; piano, doubling electronic organ, vibes and piano-accordion. Steve; clarinet, doubling tenor sax and flute. Terry; bass, doubling bass guitar. Ken; guitar, doubling electric guitar and banjo. Harry; trombone, doubling tuba and bass sax. Dick; drums, doubling vibes.

Seven jazz-orientated young men . . . with a lot of damn good musicianship shared between them.

The *Opus One* arrangement served two purposes. It showed the flair and attack of the resident jazzmen and it opened *The Venus Fly-Trap* to full business thirty minutes after the opening of the doors and while the first customers were at their tables.

It was a musical explosion. It was meant to launch the evening into full orbit. Deliberately so and one part of the club's nightly attractions.

Instead of the usual single, opening bar of fortissimo triplets, with accompanying rim-shot drum beats, Eddie Palmer's climbing trumpet scream ended with two full bars of triplets and rim-shots with the whole combo lashing out like a short machine-gun burst.

It was a signal. The door of the gaming room was opened. The table lights flicked on. Tommy and Valda Hodge made their entrance via the private door leading from the office.

It was blatant showmanship. Razzamatazz, polished and perfected enough to bring the customers back, night after night.

Thereafter Eddie Palmer and *The Opus* filled in the gaps between the various acts until two o'clock in the morning, at which point the stage show, and the club itself, closed as it had opened – with a repeat of the bomb-blasting arrangement of *Opus One*.

And on this Tuesday (as always) the gaiety and the excitement mounted as the evening wore into night and the night slipped, unobtrusively, into the small hours of the morning.

The waiters hurried between bar, kitchens and tables. Sidney Palmer, in immaculately cut evening dress, supervised the smooth delivery of drinks and food quietly from table to table, inviting and making suggestions, nipping minor complaints in the bud before they grew into open antagonism. The customer was always right – at the price he was being asked to pay he *had* to be right. And as each spat of minor annoyance was dealt with Sidney Palmer caught the eye of Hodge, and Hodge in turn strolled over to the table to chat apologetically with the occupants and, where necessary, arrange for on-the-house drinks as a means of smoothing ruffled feathers.

In short *The Venus Fly-Trap* was just about as well run an establishment as any in the United Kingdom. No strip club. No clip joint. But one of the top night-entertainment spots of the capital.

By ten o'clock every table was occupied. The gaming room was in full swing. The bar staff and the kitchen staff were preparing drinks and food as fast as they were able.

And Table Twenty-Seven was occupied.

Table Twenty-Seven. If any table could be said to be a 'special' table Table Twenty-Seven was the one. Every night – and for all night – it was reserved for two men and their various guests. Rhodes and Peters. They always wore dinner jackets, they were always immaculately groomed and they and their party *always* received slightly preferential treatment.

22

They received it and accepted it as their right.

To the hick out-of-towner, Rhodes and Peters might have been mistaken for a duo of high-spending, jet-setting, slightly-older-than-usual playboys. Men approaching their middle years, clutching what was left of their youth with fingertip determination. To the regular weekly – or monthly – patrons of *The Venus Fly-Trap* they were, perhaps, a pair of lucky guys with more money and more leisure than most.

To the police of the Big City Rhodes and Peters were two of a small army of 'untouchables'; two men hard enough to invoke terror, but smart enough to evade the law.

In the slang phraseology of their own twilight world, Rhodes and Peters were many things, but always the *same* thing. 'Leaners.' 'Frighteners.' 'Soldiers.' 'Hoods.' 'Collectors.' These and a dozen other frightening names. To those who understood they were known, respected and – where possible – given a wide berth.

And yet they didn't *look* like gangsters. Come to that, they didn't *look* like anything in particular. The truly hard men of this world rarely do; part of their terror is that they never look terrifying.

Rhodes, the quiet one, had perhaps the near-hypnotic fascination of a sleeping king cobra; the thin-lipped, unsmiling face; the drawling voice, which was never much more than a purr. But these were mere externals. Nevertheless he was, very obviously, the dominant partner. He spoke only when necessary and, more often than not, his words were disguised as moderately toned requests, but they carried the weight of orders and were always obeyed.

Peters, on the other hand, was the flashier one and seemed almost cheap and harmless by comparison. By comparison with Rhodes, that is, not by comparison with the average man. And yet . . . It was there. That 'something'. That basic lack of humanity whose absence can never be successfully hidden. Even when smiling – even when laughing – his eyes remained cold. Treachery lurked there, not too far from the surface of those eyes; treachery, cunning and naked barbarity.

Together Rhodes and Peters formed a terrifying combina-

23

tion, but the perverse nature of some women being what it is, they never lacked female companionship.

Peters' companion was a dark-haired, chic young lady, little more than a girl. Daphne Palmer. His companion this night. His companion for many nights past.

A foolish woman, even for her lack of years. A spoiled brat of a woman. Once the 'baby' of the Palmer family and now, because of the wealth and attention of her escort, pointedly ignoring the occasional presence of her worried father.

Hodge visited Table Twenty-Seven at regular intervals. The conversation, if not fawning, showed an unusual attempt to gratify.

'Everything okay, Mr Rhodes?'

Rhodes nodded.

'Mr Peters?'

'Yeah, great.'

'Miss Palmer?'

'Couldn't be better, Tommy. Couldn't be better.'

'Anything. Anything at all, just let me know.'

From the stage and from the end of the bar – when the various acts relieved *The Opus* from their place on the stage – Eddie Palmer watched the pantomime at Table Twenty-Seven. Watched and felt an unaccustomed fury boil up inside him. Scowled as he saw his kid sister pointedly insult her father; as he saw the grinning Peters encouraging the girl in her stupidity; as he saw Hodge visit the table – that table more than any other table in the room – as he saw his sister gradually become slack-limbed and glassy-eyed with a surfeit of booze.

The feeling – the fury – was alien to his make-up. It frightened him a little. But at the same time he couldn't subdue it. Couldn't even control it.

Eddie Palmer was a musician, period. The clientele of *The Venus Fly-Trap* interested him only in so far as they provided the salary necessary to keep himself and *The Opus* in business; only in so far as the tiny stage was a showcase from which they might exhibit a unique musical talent.

Nevertheless – as with all employees of such clubs – he was conscious of the fact that the very nature of the place attracted a small percentage of the more affluent scum of the capital. More than that, he was worldly enough to recognise obvious examples of that scum. To that extent he recognised Rhodes and Peters for what they were. He recognised the breed and, because of this fury inside himself, because they were in the company of his sister and, because of them, his sister was hurting his father, Eddie sought information from the wine waiter.

'Joseph. Table Twenty-Seven.'

'Yes?'

'Those two bastards with Daphne.'

'Yes?'

'Who are they?'

'Mr Rhodes and Mr Peters.'

'Thanks. And the one who can't keep his paws away from Daphne?'

'Eddie, don't . . .'

'Who is he?'

'I've – I've already told . . .'

'Which one is *he*?'

'That's . . .' The wine waiter hesitated, then said, 'That's Peters. Eddie. Wilf Peters.'

'D'you know him?'

'*Of* him.' The wine waiter stepped gingerly into dangerous territory.

'And?'

'Er – not a man to cross.'

'Is that a fact?'

'Leave him, Eddie,' advised the wine waiter gently.

'I'm not touching him, yet.'

'Eddie, he's a . . .' The wine waiter stopped.

'Yeah, he's a what? Other than somebody who makes you mess your underpants?'

'That's not fair, Eddie. I'm only trying to . . .'

'Okay. Tell me this. The rumours. The rumours that never quite reach pop's ears. Or my ears. Daphne's place at Putney.'

25

'What – what rumours?'

'Does Peters foot the bill?'

'Eddie, please don't ask me to . . .'

'Does he?' snapped Eddie.

'I – I think so.' The wine waiter nodded.

'Nice guy,' mused Eddie. 'Very generous . . . eh?'

'Eddie?' groaned the wine waiter softly. 'I'm your father's friend. I'm your friend.'

'Yeah, I know. We both know.'

'Don't cross Peters. *Please.*'

'Why?'

'It's – it's . . .'

'Doesn't he bleed?' asked Eddie flatly.

'For God's . . .'

'Doesn't he?'

'Sure.' The wine waiter nodded sadly. 'Like everybody else on earth he bleeds.'

'He will,' promised Eddie.

The wine waiter closed his eyes in silent desperation, then went about his business. Eddie stayed at the bar until the folk singer had ended her spot, then, with the members of *The Opus*, once more went on stage to make jazz for the customers until it was time for the next speciality act.

At five minutes to midnight he saw Peters help Daphne to her feet and watched the two of them walk into the gaming room.

Wednesday, June 14th

The Beetle was parked in the shadow of the trees bordering Putney Heath. Eddie Palmer was slumped low in the driver's seat, chain-smoking cigarettes and waiting. Waiting and wondering. Wondering and perhaps feeling the touch of those first fingers of doubt.

The non-violent man, jockeyed into a position where violence was a near-certainty. The truly violent man – the man who actually *enjoys* violence and especially street violence – is not as common as the newsrags would have us believe. He is a spin-off of the human race. A 'rogue' of an otherwise peaceful species. His activities are 'bad news': *ergo* he claims far more newsprint than the normal man.

But the normal man, the man typified by Eddie Palmer. What he knows of violence compares with (say) what he knows of Greek mythology. He's read about it in newspapers and in works of fiction. He's seen moving shadows of it on television and cinema screens. Since leaving school, since the days of wrestling and punching in some playground, he has taught himself to subdue a natural instinct until that instinct has become a nothing . . . until 'civilised conduct' has taken over and the natural urge towards violence against what he loathes has vanished.

And when a situation arises in which violence is an immediate and near-certain factor he has a strange and uncomfortable fear. Not the fear born of cowardice. Not even the fear of possible pain or wounding. But rather a fear that he has rejected a certain aggression which – albeit subconsciously – *should* be part of masculinity and that without that aggression the coming battle is as good as lost.

Thus Eddie Palmer. Waiting, and a little afraid.

But what the hell?

Daphne was his sister and somebody had to do *something*.

27

The dumb little bitch had to be saved from her own stupidity. That was the main thing. And if Tommy Hodge didn't like the idea of him leaving Steve to front *The Opus* for a couple of hours, Tommy Hodge could do the other thing; Tuesday night wasn't a big night at *The Fly-Trap* and everybody was entitled to plead toothache once in a while.

As for the old man . . .

Jesus. Somebody had to do *something*!

Nevertheless . . .

Joseph, the wine waiter, knew these germs. Knew what they were capable of. And, no doubt about it, Joseph had been scared. But, y'know, get first crack in. That much was obvious. Knock the bastard sideways with the first wallop, then don't give him time to get organised. Head down and in and keep punching; one good right, then wade in and keep wading in until . . .

Put that way it sounded easy.

Maybe too easy because . . .

The Merc pulled in at the entrance to the flats.

Eddie opened the door of the V.W., flicked the half-smoked cigarette on to the road surface, closed the car door, took a couple of deep breaths, then walked to where Daphne and Peters were tooling around locking the Merc for the night.

Eddie said, 'Hey . . . Peters.'

He spoke in a low voice, a slightly hoarse voice.

'What the . . .'

Peters turned. Swiftly. Smoothly. As if he was used to these situations.

Eddie cleared his throat and said, 'Just the two of us, bastard.'

He watched Peters's hands. Watched for the first sign of movement.

He added, 'A little matter of the girl you think you're taking to bed.'

'Aah!' Peters grinned. 'Your girl-friend? Your . . .'

'My sister.'

Already Eddie knew he'd made the first mistake. He'd advertised his presence too soon. Before he was within hitting

28

distance. Okay . . . he'd still get the first punch home.

He said, 'I don't like the company she keeps.'

Recognition narrowed Peters's eyes and he said, 'The punk who plays the horn at . . .'

'It's not important.'

'So? What *is* important, punk?'

'Just that you keep your paws away from one kid who's young enough to be your daughter.'

'This bint?'

'My sister.'

'Or?'

'Or this.'

It might have both started and ended the fight. The bunched fist of his right hand had every ounce of muscle Eddie could muster and it was travelling, top speed, towards the button.

With ninety-nine out of every hundred guys it would have been the decider, but Peters was part of the remaining one per cent. He swayed back, blocked the punch, then lashed into the pit of Eddie's stomach with his own right. As Eddie folded forward Peters brought up a knee to meet the face and Eddie just – and *only* just – turned his head aside and took the oncoming knee against the shoulder.

Twice more Eddie swung haymakers and, each time, they were parried and Peters's fist drove home.

Then as he crumpled, Eddie gasped, 'The mouth. Not the mouth, for Christ's sake *not the mouth.*'

Peters chuckled, glanced at the wide-eyed girl and from that moment made it a coldly scientific beat-up.

Eddie curled himself into a ball, shielded his face and as much of his head as possible with his folded arms, and clenched his teeth to keep back the screams. The beat-up was a 'boot' job; Eddie was not allowed to regain his feet; Peters lashed at the passive body with the toe, back-heeled and stamped; each blow was aimed and delivered expertly and with the open contempt of the professional for the amateur.

To Eddie it seemed to last forever.

The girl watched. She seemed hardly to breathe. Her only

29

movement was to raise her right hand to her mouth and bite hard upon the knuckle of her forefinger.

The beat-up ended. Much like an artist admiring his latest masterpiece, Peters stepped back and stared at the quietly moaning Eddie. Then without a word he turned, fastened his fingers upon the girl's upper arm and led her to the door of the flat. Once she glanced back at her injured brother, beyond that she offered no resistance.

Sidney Palmer awaited the return of his son. He knew and what he didn't know he guessed; his friend the wine waiter had mentioned Eddie's interest in the man Peters and Hodge had complained about Eddie's sudden attack of toothache. Therefore – and knowing his son – he knew, or guessed.

He sat in the darkened living room of the house in Poplar, smoked cigarettes, sipped tea, waited and worried.

These men. Strictly speaking they weren't *men*. They were animals. They were beasts who stalked a jungle of their own creation. What to them was normality sickened ordinary people. They could murder almost off-handedly. As a means of stressing a point. As a means of removing some slight irritation. As a means of brushing aside a nuisance.

Eddie didn't know. Eddie's world was one of music; he lived for jazz and jazz was his whole life. Therefore he didn't know. He could never understand – he could never be made to understand – that to these men brotherly love, brotherly concern, was a mere weakness – and not even that. Something to laugh at. Something to sneer at. Something which, if it got in the way, would be 'removed'.

It was almost three o'clock when he heard the familiar sound of the Beetle's engine; heard the gear-change, heard the switch-off, heard the car door close. He pushed himself from the chair, walked across the room and switched on the light.

He walked into the tiny hall and stood waiting for his son.

The outer door opened and for a moment the two men stood staring at each other. Then Eddie pushed the door closed behind him, leaned his back against the panels and lowered his head on to his chest. Tears welled and ran down his bruised and bloodstained cheeks.

'Eddie! Eddie!' Sidney Palmer spoke the name of his son in little more than a groan of anguish.

There was nothing the elder man could do. Wisdom after the event wouldn't ease the hurt. It wouldn't lessen the younger man's embarrassment. It wouldn't stem the sudden tears. It would do nothing. Therefore, although he yearned to turn back the clock and take his son in his arms and comfort him as he'd done as a child, Sidney Palmer contented himself with speaking Eddie's name in a tone which left no doubt that he, too, felt pain.

Eddie brushed his eyes with the heel of his hand, straightened and walked into the hall, past his father and into the living room.

'You shouldn't have,' began Palmer. 'When Joseph told me . . .'

'Forget it, pop.' Eddie lowered himself gingerly into an armchair. 'We learn things . . . that's all.'

'*Is* that all?' sighed Palmer.

'The hard way.' Eddie forced a grin.

'As long as you *do* learn.'

'Some of us aren't as tough as we think we are. Sometimes it's not that easy.'

'Your face.' Palmer touched the bruised cheek gently. 'Anywhere else?'

'Yeah.' Eddie nodded wearily. 'The guts, the shins, one of the knees and the side. I think maybe a cracked rib.'

'A doctor . . .' began Palmer.

'No doctor.' Eddie's jaw tightened. 'The bastard can't put me on my back.'

'For God's sake, Eddie.'

'Eight o'clock tonight I'm at *The Fly-Trap*. Re-varnished and as good as new.'

'That's madness.'

'Pop,' pleaded Eddie. 'Otherwise the bastard's beaten me.'

'And *hasn't* he?' asked Palmer sadly.

'The first round,' murmured Eddie.

31

'Eddie, don't start being . . .'

'Oh, no! There'll be another round. One more round. Then . . .'

'Eddie, please see . . .'

'No, pop.' The rage was deep. Smouldering. 'One more round. Another day. And I'll cool him. I swear. I'll cool that bloody animal forever.'

By late afternoon it was known. How? Nobody could satisfactorily answer that question. The drums of Africa have nothing on the silent telegraph system of the underworld: nods, winks and whispers; half-smiles and raised eyebrows; part of the criminal sign language. Eddie Palmer had had a going over. Eddie Palmer had strayed into forbidden territory. Eddie Palmer was a punk, a dumb punk who was now wiser than he'd been this time yesterday.

Sidney Palmer went about the pattern of preparation, quietly and with his usual gentle dignity. He hid his worry as much as he was able, but those who knew him could see the sadness at the back of his eyes. The slight stoop to his shoulders. The distinct effort necessary for his usual concentration.

Valda Hodge touched his arm and led him to a quiet corner of the room.

She said, 'I heard about last night.'

'Ma'am?' Sidney pretended not to understand.

'About Eddie taking a beating.'

'Bad news travels fast,' said Sidney sadly.

Valda glanced at the stage, at where *The Opus* were setting up their instruments, fingering chords and jazz figures, tuning up and exchanging small talk.

She said, 'Will he be in?'

'Later.'

'Oh!' She sounded surprised.

'He shouldn't.' Mild defiance touched Sidney's tone. 'He's been hurt badly. Why should *he* worry?'

'Pride,' suggested Valda.

'Proud . . . to have been kicked almost unconscious?'
Bitterness joined the defiance.

'Be proud of him, Sidney,' she said softly.

He gave no answer.

She said, 'About Daphne. That's what I hear.'

'Yes.'

'And Peters.'

He nodded.

'That's bad.' The compassion in her voice was genuine.
'I'm sorry. That's . . . bad.'

Sidney said, 'The boss could have stopped it. He could
have put a ban on Daphne, then . . .'

'It's not that easy,' she interrupted.

'If he'd refuse her admission.'

'And Peters?' she asked gently.

There was no answer.

'And Rhodes?' she added.

'I – I don't see what . . .'

'Mobsters. Haven't you guessed?'

'That's none of my business.'

'It is now. With Eddie.'

'Just to ban Daphne. That's all,' he muttered.

'No.' She shook her head sadly. 'Now it's Eddie.'

'But they don't *own* this place.'

'No?' It was perhaps meant to be a simple statement. But
the rise of her voice turned it into a question.

'Do they?' Sidney's words *were* a question. Blunt. Shocked.

'Not yet,' she sighed.

'Y'mean . . .'

'Not yet. Maybe never.' Her mood changed; as if she was
angry with herself for saying fractionally too much. She
said, 'Get with it, Sidney. Little men dancing to strings pulled
by big men. That's the game we all play. And the strings
mustn't get tangled.'

'And Daphne's caught up in those strings?'

'Could be. I'm sorry . . . she won't be the first. Or the last.'

Valda ended the conversation abruptly by turning and
walking away. Sidney Palmer stared after her. Worry and

fear creased his expression. Dear God, he was a waiter. Nothing more. A head waiter. A *good* head waiter, and that was all he was. That was all he wanted to be. To be left alone, to be just that.

The nature of his job – the nature of his place of work – brought him within touching distance of men who were part of London's mobs. Him and a thousand other men and women employed at similar work, in similar places. But you built a wall. An invisible wall. If you had any sense you built a wall, and you never tried to scale that wall. You never even tried to look over it. You stayed on one side, they stayed on the other. You served them . . . that was your job. You served them, you made sure they enjoyed their meals – their nights out – but beyond that nothing. Not if you'd any sense.

Unless, of course, you had a daughter . . .

Unless, of course, you had a son . . .

Outside London flexed its muscles for the start of one more daily exodus; the homeward-bound rush hour when pavements, roads, the Underground and railway stations swarmed with frustrated travellers and humanity resembled panic-stricken bees in a disturbed hive.

Freda Palmer left the Tube at Southfields. From there she walked, almost elbowing her way past other pavement-users, oblivious to everything other than the need to visit this brainless brat of a daughter of hers and demand an explanation.

Her friends – what few friends she allowed herself – would have been surprised at the thrust of her chin. She was known for her tranquillity. For her even temper. For the very few times she'd been known to even raise her voice.

But on this June afternoon the anger could be seen in the tightness of her lips and the glint in her eyes.

She thumbed the bell-push and Daphne's voice was distorted by the speaker alongside the door.

'Who is it?'

'Your mother.'

'What do you want?'

'Open the door, girl. I've no intention of standing here talking to you through this silly contraption.'

'I . . .' There was a pause. 'I don't want to talk to you, mother.'

Freda Palmer moved her mouth nearer to the grille of the microphone-cum-speaker and snapped, 'Open this door, girl. Either for me or for a policeman.'

There was another pause, then Daphne's voice said, 'Okay. Come on up. It's open.'

Freda Palmer turned the knob, pushed open the door, stalked through the hall and climbed the stairs to the flat.

The two women faced each other on the threshold of the flat door. Staid middle age opposing the good-time girl wearing a little too much make-up. Simmering anger opposing petulance.

For a moment they glared at each other.

Then Daphne stepped aside and said, 'Well? *Are* you coming in? Or have you climbed the stairs for nothing?'

'So, this is it?' The elder woman stepped into the room and turned her head to survey the expensive gaudiness. Her mouth curled as she added, 'All this for whoredom?'

'Mother, I'm not going to stand here and . . .'

'You're going to listen, girl.' The mother's eyes gleamed fury. 'You're going to listen to something that should have been said years ago. It's too late, but it's still going to be said.'

'Look, just because Eddie . . .'

'Yes. Let's talk about Eddie.' Without being invited the elder woman flopped into one of the armchairs. 'Let's talk about your brother. He should be in hospital. At the very least he should be in bed. One of your clients did that to him. One of the men . . .'

'He's not a "client",' flared Daphne. 'I'm not a tart. I'm not a prostitute.'

'What else do you do?' mocked the mother. 'Sing to them?'

'I didn't ask Eddie to . . .'

'From what I hear you didn't ask your boy-friend to stop either.'

'Mother, you don't understand.'

'Do *you*?'

'I couldn't have . . .'

'When you were young.' The mother whiplashed the girl with her tongue. Almost spat the words out. 'When you were young. A snivelling little schoolgirl like a frightened mouse. Eddie fought for you. He was your brother, still is your brother. In those days you ran to him for protection and he never let you down. Not once. You were a stupid, brainless little cow in *those* days. You still are.'

'I'm a grown woman.' The girl's voice was harsh with outraged fury.

'You're a nothing. A *nothing*!' Freda Palmer waved her hand. 'This. This fine living. This fancy flat. You've earned it like every other tart on earth earns things. On your back.'

'For Christ's sake. I'll not stand here and listen to . . .'

'You'll listen, girl. I've come here to make you listen. And, by God, you *will* listen. They don't know I'm here. Your father, Eddie, they don't know I've come here. This is *my* idea. So get your fine friend to kick *me* to death.'

'Mother, don't be mad. Don't . . .'

'Just to tell you this. Just to let you know.' Freda Palmer pushed herself from the armchair. She pointed a stiffened finger at her daughter as she rasped, 'At birth. As long ago as that. You were a damn nuisance. You gave me pain, pain you'll never understand. But that would have been worth it. Everything would have been worth it, if you'd even been half-decent. Your father. He's worked every hour God sends . . . for you. All his life. Doting on you. Doting on a little bitch like *you*! You couldn't do wrong. *You,* who couldn't do right! You were special to him. Did you ever know that? Did you ever realise that? Special. To him and to Eddie.'

'But not to you?' The girl's face was made ugly by contempt.

'No, never to me. A woman knows another woman . . . even when she's only a child.'

'And I'm a big girl now.'

36

'You think you are.'

'I could buy and sell you.'

'I'm not for sale, girl, something you wouldn't understand.'

'Wilf says I'm his lucky charm,' taunted the girl.

'I don't know anybody called "Wilf". Or want to.'

'Wilf Peters.'

'One of the hooligans you go to bed with?'

'With me at the table he can't go wrong.'

'You're lower than dog dirt, girl. D'you know that?'

'Three nights in a row.'

'I'm not interested.'

'*Be* interested,' mocked the girl. 'The winnings. You wouldn't believe the winnings.'

'From you? I wouldn't believe a damn thing.'

'He says he'll buy me a sports car if his luck holds.'

'Oh, for heaven's sake . . .'

'I'm lucky, ma. That's what upsets you all. I'm lucky. I've dragged myself out of that Poplar dump. You – Eddie, father – you'll all rot and die there. But not me. I've bettered myself. I've made a life for . . .'

'*Shut up!*' Freda Palmer almost screamed the words. Her whole frame trembled as she fought to control her rage. Then, in little more than a whisper, she said, 'Shut up, girl. If you value those eyes of yours, shut up.'

'Okay.' Daphne nodded. 'So why did you come here?'

'Why?'

'I'm not going back home with you, if that's what you think. I'm not . . .'

'I wouldn't let you soil my carpets,' breathed Freda.

'Okay. Why come?'

'Eddie.'

'Damn Eddie. I don't *care* about Eddie. I don't care about *any* of you.'

'That's – that's why I'm here.'

'It's been a wasted journey then, hasn't it?'

'Eddie's been hurt. Hurt badly.'

'Eddie asked for it. He shouldn't have . . .'

'He oughtn't to be alone.'

37

'Look, what the hell . . .'

The fear in the girl's voice was too late. She screamed as the elder woman took a step forward and, with a full-blooded back-handed swing, hurled her right fist at the girl's face. The blow landed flush on the right eye, then bounced off the nose and the girl toppled backwards, tripped and sprawled on the carpet.

Freda Palmer stared down at her sobbing daughter. For a moment it looked as if she might spit on the girl.

Then she said, 'You know where I live. Send your man-friend round if you want me to do the same to him. Don't get up, I'll let myself out.'

At eight o'clock Eddie Palmer ripped the glissando opening out of his horn, and led the combo into *Opus One*. The bruised muscles of his face throbbed in protest, but he forced his mind to ignore the pain. The pain in his face was only part of the pain which seemed to wrap itself around his whole body. His side. His shoulders. His chest. Even his leg.

But to hell with the pain. Upright he remained undefeated. On the stand, leading the combo, he was not merely unde-feated . . . he was the victor.

Peters had to be made to understand this.

Stage make-up and tinted sunglasses hid the bruises. The pain didn't matter a damn. Given time the pain would go away. But pride? That was another thing altogether. The good guys tamed the bad guys . . . always. The book of words said so. The good guys eventually made the bad guys look creeps. All it needed was guts.

And . . .

Everybody at *The Venus Fly-Trap* – from Tommy Hodge down – knew about last night's beat-up. Everybody knew the size of it. The reason for it. The name of the bastard who'd delivered it. Everybody knew just about everything, and that, too, helped.

It helped make Peters look small.

The boys in the outfit had known.

Paul had said, 'The easy numbers tonight, Eddie.'

'What easy numbers?' Eddie's question had been harsh. Challenging.

'Low register. Slow. Not too many high notes.'

'Forget it, Paul.'

'Look, man, I understand. I dig all the reasons. But if you blow high and play a fart he's gonna . . .'

'You handle the keyboards. Okay? I stand in front and blow the horn. Fast and high. Tonight is no different.'

'You'll poop,' Paul had said sadly.

Eddie had growled, 'If I poop – just once – I walk off that stage and somebody else fronts you.'

'Okay.' Paul had shrugged resignedly. 'If *I* hit any wrong ones, you'll know why. I'll be keeping my fingers crossed.'

And after that stage make-up and tinted sunglasses, and that was all. And everybody in *The Fly-Trap* knew; some were silently rooting for him and some thought he was a swollen-headed fool and some suffered with him and some didn't give a damn. Who cared? This was strictly between himself and Peters with that stupid little bint, Daphne, an interested onlooker. Nobody else mattered. This was a very private war.

It was a little after nine o'clock before Peters, Rhodes and Daphne walked into the main room. Peters glanced at the stage, saw Eddie and, perhaps for a second more than was necessary, continued to look. His face was expressionless as he returned his attention to the girl and guided her towards Table Twenty-Seven.

Daphne, too, was wearing dark glasses. Quite a few shades darker than those worn by Eddie.

Alongside him Harry eased the slide of his trombone and murmured, 'Snap,' but Eddie ignored the remark.

Daphne's face was swollen and showed discoloration below the frames of the spectacles. Very deliberately she kept her face turned away from the stage.

As the trio walked towards the table Rhodes looked directly at Eddie. Nothing moved about his face, his mouth remained its usual thin-lipped slit, but the impression was that he was enjoying sardonic amusement. It was in his eyes. The heavyweight champ watching two amateur flyweights playing at being tough.

From their station near the bar Sidney Palmer and his friend Joseph, the wine waiter, watched the tiny pantomime.

'It shouldn't happen, Sidney,' murmured Joseph.

Sidney raised a hand, snapped his fingers to attract the attention of one of the waiters and pointed to Table Twenty-Seven.

Joseph said, 'Daphne. You think Peters, perhaps?'

'She doesn't tell me things.'

'Men like him knock their womenfolk around sometimes.'

'It's possible,' sighed Sidney.

'I'm sorry, old friend.'

Sidney nodded.

Up on the stage the combo ended a number. Eddie turned and said, 'Okay . . . *Blueberry Hill.*'

'Hey, man,' warned Harry, 'don't try for that Armstrong chorus.'

'As always.' said Eddie grimly.

'For Christ's sake!'

'You feel like leading this outfit?'

'Hey, kid, I'm your friend . . . remember?'

'Okay. After four. *Blueberry Hill.* With the Armstrong chorus.'

It was a gesture. It took some playing. That third chorus with all the high-flying trumpet work, lifted from the Armstrong recording, left him limp and sweating. But it was necessary. Okay, Peters made believe he couldn't see, but sure as hell he could *hear*. He had to be *made* to hear. A so-called tough guy gives a common-or-garden horn blower the order of the boot, and that horn man can still hit and hold the high ones. That tough baby isn't *so* damn tough.

The closing sizzle cymbal from Dick came like a prayer, and his head felt as if it was dancing up and down on a coil spring. But he made it and, as always, there was a ripple of applause. Even Rhodes clapped, but maybe not at the music.

It was just after eleven o'clock – Eddie and *The Opus*

40

were nearing their second session on stage – when the three men strolled down the steps from the entrance and stood to one side of the door of the dining-cum-concert-room. Three men; three of a kind. The two outer men were taller and more broad-shouldered than their companion. They flanked him protectively. Their eyes were never still. They were, in mobster parlance, 'soldiers'; they were on duty; tight-muscled and ready to explode into action.

The man in the middle smoked a cigarette and he, too, examined the room and its occupants, much as a parasitologist might examine interesting organisms. With mild curiosity, touched with expertise.

Sidney Palmer saw the trio and walked across the room towards them. One of the flanking men flipped a hand and dismissed Palmer without a word.

The man in the middle caught Rhodes's eye. He moved his head, ever so slightly, and Rhodes pushed back his chair, stood up from the table and joined the trio.

'Well?'

The voice of the man in the middle was little more than a croaking whisper. The voice of a man with a serious throat defect.

'You can see,' said Rhodes.

'Yeah.'

'It's like this most nights.'

'No trouble?'

'No trouble at all.'

'That's not what *I* hear,' croaked the man in the middle.

'Peters?' murmured Rhodes.

'The trumpet man.'

Rhodes said, 'Peters is a fink.'

'Yeah.' The man in the middle glanced at Table Twenty-Seven. 'The kid with the shades?'

'Peters likes her.'

'Yeah?'

'She lets him keep her bed warm.'

'Tell him,' croaked the man in the middle.

'What?'

41

'Ditch her . . . fast.'

'Sure.'

'He's not paid to screw school-kids.'

'I'll tell him.'

'And keep me posted.'

'Sure.'

'You . . . not Peters.'

'Sure.'

'Okay. Blow.'

Rhodes returned to Table Twenty-Seven. For a few moments the man with the croaking voice watched the occupants of the dining-cum-concert-room. Then without a word he turned and left, flanked by his two 'soldiers'.

Thursday, June 15th

A new day arrived with the short hiccup of a second hand; for a splinter of time the hour hand and the minute hand kissed at midnight, then it was a new day. A new day, but part of the old night. Few people at *The Venus Fly-Trap* – staff or customers – noticed Thursday take over from Wednesday. It happened while they were taking a drink, while they were chatting, while they watched the ivory ball spin around the rim of a roulette wheel, while they gave some small attention to the girl on stage who was stroking the strings of a guitar and musically bemoaning the loss of recent love. Eternity lengthened itself by one more day, but few people were aware of it.

In one of the tiny dressing rooms beyond the stage Eddie Palmer slumped in a cane chair, smoked a cigarette, tried to accept his pain without mock-heroism and, at the same time, tried not to feel sorry for himself.

It would have been very easy to indulge himself in self-pity. It would have been *too* easy.

That *Blueberry Hill* thing. A crazy gesture. More than that, an empty gesture. That damn number was out – but *out*! – until the pain in his side eased. A cracked rib? Yeah, maybe a cracked rib, that wouldn't be too hard to believe. Just breathing wasn't too comfortable. Deep breathing was distinctly painful. And using your lungs like bellows to squeeze out those long-held high notes, Jesus, that had been pure agony. And for what? To prove what?

That sloppy kid sister of his had lost her marbles. What's more she didn't give a back-of-the-hand damn. Last night she'd done nothing. Nothing! She'd stood there and watched. Not a peep. Not a single objection, while Peters had been kicking ten shades of shit out of her own brother. Daphne, eh? The panicky little kid who'd messed her panties if some

43

snotty-nosed tyke as much as shoved his tongue out at her. Panicked and raced around finding 'her Eddie'. Jesus Christ! People could change. Nice people . . . they could change into real bastards.

The door of the dressing room opened and Sidney Palmer entered.

Eddie grinned ruefully and said, 'Hiya, pop.'

'How do you feel?' Sidney closed the door and scrutinised his son's face anxiously.

'Just so long as nobody asks for a four-minute mile,' said Eddie.

'Seen Daphne's face?' asked Sidney.

'Not close up. I see she's wearing Polaroids.'

'She's bruised,' said Sidney sadly.

'Great.'

'Eddie!' protested the elder man.

'Hey, pop.' Eddie spoke solemnly. 'Me, too, I'm bruised . . . remember? Because of *that* little cow.'

'I know, but . . .'

'Yeah, I know. Gentlemen don't belt women. Okay. Chances are she spoke out of turn to Peters. Okay, now she knows he's *not* a gentleman.'

Sidney Palmer sighed. Some things he didn't understand. Some things he didn't *want* to understand – they were of no interest to him – but some of the things he'd have liked to understand, he still didn't understand. The experts who wrote about these things – who lectured about them on the radio and the television – talked about 'The Generation Gap'. It was a phrase. To Sidney Palmer it had no meaning. A family was a family; parents, children, maybe grandchildren. 'Gaps' didn't make sense. A family with 'gaps' wasn't a proper family. Somebody had made a big mistake somewhere. Somebody had taught false values. A man loved his wife, loved his kids and in return, as a reward for that love. *he* was loved. The rest didn't matter. The music, the books, the films, the relaxation of morals. That was all surface stuff. That could be accepted – not understood, but accepted – just as long as the *family* stayed in one piece.

44

Eddie said, 'You've seen the lice she calls "friends"?'

'I know,' muttered Sidney.

'Hodge could slam the door. Dammit, he could . . .'

'Hodge has his own worries,' said Sidney gently.

'Eh?'

'Valda Hodge dropped hints. I don't think she meant to, they just slipped out.'

'Hints?'

'I'm only guessing.' Sidney hesitated, then added, 'I don't think it'll be his door to slam for much longer.'

'What the . . .' Eddie stared.

'You saw them.'

'Who?'

'No, maybe not.' Sidney moved his shoulders.

'Who?' repeated Eddie.

'The man.'

'What man?'

In a weary voice Sidney said, 'They don't have a name, son. People like us aren't told, they never have a name. They have money. And power. And ways of getting their own way.'

'The mobs?' Eddie moistened his lips.

Sidney didn't answer.

'The mobs?' insisted Eddie. 'Is that what you're talking about?'

'One of them looked in this evening.' Sidney's voice was flat. Dull. Unemotional. 'One of them with the bodyguard.'

'When?' Eddie screwed what was left of his cigarette into an ashtray.

'You weren't meant to notice.'

'Oh!'

'Nobody was meant to notice. I don't think many people did. But I see things. It's part of my job.'

Eddie said, 'Pop, what gives? What goes on? I mean . . .'

'I've lived in this world longer than you, Eddie.' Sidney drew the palms of his hands down each side of his face; as if wiping away some of the wretchedness; as if removing self-imposed blinkers. He said, 'Little things. Signs. They're there

45

if you know what to look for. Rhodes. At a guess, Peters. They're of a kind. They're keeping an eye on things.'

'Peters?'

Sidney nodded.

'And – and Daphne?'

'She won't be warned. She believes what she wants to believe. She won't listen. So, she'll learn, but she'll get hurt.'

'Peters, eh?' Eddie's voice was harsh with hatred. His previous disgust at his sister was forgotten. He said, 'Okay. I'll get *him* off her back.'

'No!' It was almost a moan of despair. 'Not both of you. They're bad men, Eddie. Evil men. Believe me.'

Eddie glanced at his watch and said, 'We're due on the stand, pop.'

'Eddie . . .'

'Sorry.' Eddie pushed himself from the chair; winced as the movement brought a stab of pain.

'Eddie, for God's sake don't . . .'

'Bad men, eh? Hard men? I just wonder *how* hard.'

Thursday, June 22nd

Another day. Another Thursday. Indeed, another week. June was edging its way towards full summer; the bleak days of winter were almost a forgotten memory and already office workers were enjoying lunch breaks on the grass of the capital.

It was mid-afternoon and south of the river at Putney Daphne Palmer was almost speechless with joy.

'It's yours, kid,' grinned Peters. 'A man has luck at the tables. He has to make sure that luck stays with him.'

'It's – it's . . .'

She stroked the gloss of the cream paintwork.

'Try it,' suggested Peters. 'It's as fast as it looks.'

It was, too. It was low-slung and wide wheel-based. It was open and built for high-speed travelling along the motorways and autobahns. It was the personification of jet-propelled youth.

'Try it,' repeated Peters.

'Now?' There was wide-eyed wonderment in the girl's eyes.

'Sure, why not? It's taxed, juiced up and raring to go.' Peters held the car door open. 'See what she'll do. I'll be around to pick you up some time after eight.'

'Can't – can't you go with me?'

'No way, kid.' Peters's grin turned to a sad smile. 'I have things to do. You take off. Enjoy yourself.'

She did, too. South on the A3; past Wimbledon Common; along the Kingston by-pass; past Sandown Park Racecourse and on towards Claremont Park. It was a beautiful car. A touch on the accelerator and it surged forward, as if eager to demonstrate the blue-blooded power of every horse under its bonnet. Sixty was a mere cruising speed. Eighty demanded

47

little more than slight extra pressure with the right foot. The few times she touched a three-figure speed on the straight stretches of road seemed to make the magnificent engine catch her own exhilaration and throw it back at her in the slip-stream which streamered her hair.

She did as Peters had suggested. She enjoyed herself.

For perhaps an hour she enjoyed herself, then she and the beautiful car died. Together. In a moment and in a mass of screaming, tortured metal, screeching rubber and shattering glass; they – both she and the car – spilled themselves on the surface of the road for a distance of more than fifty yards.

At *The Venus Fly-Trap* Sidney Palmer went about his duties with a lighter heart. His daughter Daphne was absent from Table Twenty-Seven. Rhodes was there. Peters was there. But on this night Peters had a new companion; a brassy, auburn-haired good-timer, nearer his own age than Daphne.

Joseph, the wine waiter, also noticed.

In one of their moments of relaxation, Joseph said, 'I'm happy for you, Sidney.'

'I'm happy, too.' Sidney Palmer smiled.

'Could be she'll come back. Come to her senses.'

'She's my daughter, Joseph.'

'Sure.'

'My home is *her* home.'

'Sure that's what I mean.'

Valda Hodge also noticed. She cornered her husband and said, 'She's not here tonight.'

'Who?' Tommy Hodge pretended not to understand.

'For Christ's sake.'

'Oh, you mean the Palmer kid?'

'Who else?'

'Maybe Peters has ditched her.'

'You think so?'

'How the hell do I know?'

'Hey, hubby,' warned Valda softly, 'don't get jumpy with *me*. Anybody else . . . go right ahead. But ride *me* gently. Otherwise . . .'

48

Even Eddie noticed and it made his night. The pain from the beat-up was now little more than a memory-jogging twinge and this, coupled with Daphne's absence from Table Twenty-Seven, made his horn playing high and happy.

Indeed, many customers and staff of *The Venus Fly-Trap* observed the absence of Peters's usual companion. Some merely noticed and dismissed the observation from their mind. Others remarked upon it.

But not Peters.

Peters had found a new plaything . . . he couldn't have cared less.

Friday, June 23rd

There is, in fact, an eighth 'deadly sin'. Optimism. The stupid habit of taking one simple fact and, from that, building a cloud-high edifice of wishful thinking. And more than that. Disregarding all other probabilities and instead reaching a conclusion which in time becomes *the* conclusion. The only conclusion.

By two-thirty in the morning of that June Friday – by the time the members of *The Opus* had ended the minor chores necessary after a night's session – Sidney and Eddie Palmer had convinced themselves. Their combined optimism had done the trick.

Eddie said, 'She'll be there, pop. She'll be there and waiting.'

'Be kind to her.' A tiny furrow of worry touched Sidney's forehead.

'Sure. Why not?'

'Y'know . . .' Sidney forced a smile. 'What Peters did. Don't blame Daphne.'

'No way, pop.' Eddie touched his father's arm affectionately. 'No way.'

Joseph, the wine waiter, had volunteered to stand in for Sidney and supervise the final clearing away. Hodge had raised no objections. Therefore Sidney sat in the front passenger seat of the V.W. Beetle as Eddie drove it east from the city towards Poplar.

Within the confines of the tiny car the two men seemed to draw closer. They were more than father and son. They were also friends; happy friends about to share a glorious moment. The age gap disappeared. The sheer joy of anticipation overrode all other emotions.

Eddie said. 'Back together again, eh?'

'A complete family.'

50

'The Palmers against the world.'

'Eddie . . .' The elder man seemed to have difficulty in finding the right words. He muttered, 'You're a good boy, Eddie.'

'Hey, pop.' Eddie grinned to hide his embarrassment. 'Save it for Daphne. Make *her* feel good, too.'

They reached Poplar and Sidney waited until Eddie had parked and locked the V.W.; waited, as if unwilling to savour that first moment of choking happiness alone; as if wishing to magnify it by sharing it with the younger man.

They entered the house together. Together they walked into the lighted living room . . . and together they felt the joy evaporate.

Freda Palmer was sitting on the edge of an armchair, on the very edge, with her elbows resting on her knees and her sunken eyes staring into nothingness. Her fingers were locked together in front of her lap; locked together and seemingly trying to tie themselves into impossible knots. Her face was without expression, but pale as if it had never known the warmth of blood.

She seemed unaware of their entry.

Eddie hurried across the room. placed an arm across the bowed shoulders and said, 'Ma. Hey, ma. What's happened?'

She didn't answer. She didn't move. She didn't seem to hear.

Sidney joined his son and said, 'Freda. Pet. Are you ill or something? What's the . . .'

'Daphne's dead.'

She moved her bloodless lips long enough to say the two words. Softly. Without sorrow. Without anger. Without any show of emotion at all.

There was a silence. A complete silence; so intense that the sound of distant, small-hour traffic could be heard.

Sidney moistened his lips and whispered, 'Wh-what are you saying, Freda? What – what . . .'

'Ma.' Eddie's voice was little more than a groan. 'Ma, you're wrong. You *have* to be wrong.'

'No.' She moved her head slowly and looked at her son.

51

She muttered, 'She died thinking we hated her. Thinking *I* hated her.'

'No, ma. That's not true. She – she knew . . .'

'I hit her,' droned the woman. 'Last week. I went there. I called her foul names. Terrible names. Then – then I hit her. Knocked her down before I left.' She raised her face and looked at her husband. 'Please, Sidney. I'm sorry. I'm so *sorry*.'

Sidney Palmer closed his eyes. Then opened them, swallowed and tried to speak, but couldn't. He nodded his head, gently, in understanding.

'Look, ma.' Eddie straightened and made an effort to clear the numbness from his mind. 'What – y'know – what happened?'

'I – I went to see her . . .'

'No. I mean now. Today.'

'He promised to buy her a car.'

'Please. I mean . . .'

'She told me. He'd buy her a car if his luck held.'

'Who?'

Suddenly for a moment the woman's tone changed. Unreasonable fury turned her expression ugly and she spat, 'Two of you. Two grown men. And you couldn't look after her. A little girl, that's all she was. A little girl. A child. And – and you couldn't save her from this.'

Then her face seemed to collapse inwards and the tears spilled over and ran down her cheeks.

'Ma.' Eddie held the narrow shoulders in a protective arc. He allowed the agony to run its course, then said, 'Ma, please. Say it. Please! Whatever it is. Just say it. Just the once. Then we'll know.'

She took a deep, shuddering breath, regained a measure of control, then muttered, 'He – he must have bought her the car.'

'Who?' asked Sidney. 'Who bought her a . . .'

'Peters.'

Eddie snarled, '*That* bloody animal.'

'Where is she now?' asked Sidney. 'At the hospital? At . . .'

'She's in a mortuary.'

'Oh, my God!' breathed Sidney.

'And the police left you like this?' Eddie's heartbreak was swamped by outrage. 'They didn't even . . .'

'They left me,' said the woman tonelessly. 'They left me. I told them to leave me. I sent them away. They wanted to notify you. I said not. I wouldn't let them notify you. I told them not to. A – a policewoman. She wanted to stay. Why? Why should *she* stay? I don't want a policewoman. I want Daphne. That's who I want. Daphne. I – I want . . .'

Then she broke down completely. The sobs tore through her body, until it became difficult for her to breathe. It was a climax; a peak of wretchedness. Self-torment. Utter misery. Heartbreak almost beyond comprehension. It was all there . . . and more.

The two men were helpless. To hold her meant nothing. To murmur their own unhappy sympathy was a waste of time.

Eddie said, 'Look after her, pop. Tea . . . with brandy. That's about all we can do, till she's cried it out.'

'What?' Sidney Palmer was almost as incapable of understanding things as his wife.

'I'll go,' said Eddie.

'What? Where?'

'The police. They'll . . . tell me where she is.'

'Oh!'

'She'll have to be seen. Identified . . . just to be sure. I'll go. You stay with ma.'

He was sent to Esher Police Station and from there was taken to a mortuary. A place of official, clinically accepted death; a cold, white-tiled, barren place, washed with the blue-tinged illumination from strip-lighting.

The constable warned him, 'There'll be an inquest, Mr Palmer.'

53

'Yeah.' Eddie nodded.

'She's – er . . .' The constable paused before he drew the sheet aside. 'Don't be too shocked, Mr Palmer.'

'No . . . okay.'

It was Daphne. Despite the shattered skull and the mangled features, it was Daphne. He tightened his jaw muscles and forced himself to look.

'Your sister?' murmured the constable.

Eddie nodded.

The constable returned the sheet and said, 'Inquest, Monday. I'd make arrangements for the funeral for Tuesday.'

'Yeah.' Eddie held himself rigid and tried to sponge the memory of the face and head from his mind. He said, 'The car? It – it wasn't hers.'

'Strictly speaking, sir.' The constable tidied the sheet. 'A chap called Peters. Wilfred Peters. He bought it *for* her.'

'Does he know?' Eddie glanced at the sheeted figure.

'He was notified. The registration number . . . we got her Putney address from that. Then the garage. The garage told us about Peters. Peters loaned us a key for the Putney flat. That's how we traced the Poplar address.' The constable hesitated, then said, 'The key . . . do *you* want it?'

'Key?'

'To the Putney flat. Presumably it must be your sister's . . .'

'No.'

'To Peters?' asked the constable tentatively.

'Yeah . . . anywhere.'

As they walked from the mortuary Eddie said, 'Look . . . it *was* an accident?'

'I'm sorry, sir. I don't . . .'

'No. It doesn't matter. Of course it was an accident.'

The constable said, 'I'm sorry, Mr Palmer. You've seen her. She was going at a hell of a lick.'

'Yeah.'

'A hell of a lick,' repeated the constable sadly.

Eddie drove the V.W. slowly and in third gear.

The delayed shock made his whole body tremble. Played

54

havoc with his concentration. He was a young man and the truth was he'd just been into a mortuary for the first time and he'd just seen his first corpse.

His brain seemed to refuse to function properly; seemed to refuse to answer his control; seemed hellbent on taking its own nightmare path of questioning. Wild thoughts – terrifying realisations – piled, one on top of the other, and seemed to cause a fog through which he had to peer at the road ahead.

Birth. Death. Dammit everybody was born. Everybody died. The two great common denominators of mankind. Of *everything*. Birth and death. But – y'know . . . how many people had witnessed a birth? Not the mother. Not the father, not those husbands who opt to be present at the birth of their own child. Not the textbook photographs or the television pictures. No, the real thing. The blood and muck and pain of birth. How many? It happened to everybody, but in some odd way secretly. Hidden. Something nobody *really* talked about.

The same with death. Bodies. Corpses. Forget undertakers – morticians – what the hell you wanted to call 'em, forget *them*. How many people like him. Adult. Not kids, but grown people and they'd never seen a dead body. Never. Some, y'know, some never *would*. Born – with all the mess and anguish of birth – then die with more mess and more anguish . . . and damn-all in between. They should be made to see. They should be *made* to look.

That thing back there. That 'thing'. Daphne? Christ, no, not *Daphne* – not *that* God-awful mess. Not that! Daphne was a living person. Okay, she was dead, but she wasn't *that*.

Nobody was *that*. Ever!

He braked the car and double-parked alongside a row of vehicles left for the night. He massaged his face to try to rid himself of the horrors which threatened to swamp him.

Dawn had arrived. Dawn over the greatest city in the world. Dawn over a city which within hours would be pulsating with life. A wet dawn, a haze of rain drifted from the lightening, metal-grey sky.

And behind him . . .

He breathed, 'Oh, Jesus!' felt in his pockets then lighted a cigarette.

He was surprised to find his cheeks moist.

Tuesday, June 27th

The tiny knot of mourners gathered outside the crematorium chapel. Such a small group, less than a dozen. Sidney, Freda and Eddie, Joseph, and Tommy and Valda Hodge, an aunt, an uncle and two cousins. So few people willing to interrupt the pattern of their daily life in order to pay a last respect to a young woman who, in her youth, had had so many friends.

Sidney Palmer gripped his wife's hand; tried to pass strength and courage via the pressure of his fingers. He knew how she felt . . . exactly how she felt. He, too, felt the same way.

The purpose-built chapel; not *really* a place of worship; not *really* a House of God. An ante-chamber to a furnace. More comfortable, perhaps, than the floor-boards around a grave. Cleaner than mounds of clay and soil. Cleaner, more comfortable, but in some strange way more off-handed. The piped music; supermarket music, geared for a specific occasion. The so-called 'service'. Droned by a strange cleric without feeling, complete with ersatz solemnity.

Whatever she'd done – however much hurt she'd given – she deserved more than *that.*

Sidney Palmer squeezed his wife's hand and murmured, 'Never mind, pet. *We* know.'

The group disintegrated. Slowly. Almost, it seemed, unwillingly. Like miscued actors and actresses who had forgotten their lines and didn't know what to say – what to do – next.

Valda Hodge muttered something to her husband, then walked towards Sidney and Freda.

She said, 'I'm sorry, Sidney. Mrs Palmer. I know . . . At a time like this everybody says the same. But I am. We both are. If there's anything we can do. Anything.'

57

Freda nodded and forced the mockery of a smile.

Valda turned, but before she reached her husband Eddie stopped her.

In a low, choked voice, he said, 'Peters.'

'Easy, boy.' Valda touched his arm comfortingly. 'You can't . . .'

'I can.' His tone was harsh and without compromise. 'And I do. As surely as if he'd slit her throat.'

'Eddie!'

'Without him she'd be here.'

'Look, it was an accident. She drove too fast. She . . .'

'Thanks to Peters.'

'He gave her a car. That's all.'

'And? Without the bloody car?'

'Eddie,' she pleaded. 'Cool it. She was your sister, mourn for her. That's right. That's as it should be. But forget Peters. He's a dangerous man. He's . . .'

'Bullet-proof?'

'Hey!' The combined tone and words startled her. She said, 'Cool it, Eddie. Okay, she was your sister. You're upset and right now . . .'

'I want a gun,' he said flatly.

'Don't look at me, friend.'

'I want a gun,' he repeated. 'I think you could get me one.'

'No way.'

'Please.'

'Look, I'm doing you a big favour.'

'The only favour I want. Get me a gun.'

'For Christ's sake, Eddie. Talk to your father. Don't go around asking people . . .'

'I'm asking you.'

'No way,' she said slowly. Deliberately.

'I thought we were friends,' he sneered.

'You don't know how much of a friend I am.'

'All I'm asking . . .'

'Don't!' Her expression showed angry disgust.

58

'Why?' The heartbroken contempt bordered upon an insult. 'Does Peters scare *you*?'

'Guns scare me,' she snapped, then turned and joined her husband.

As they drove back towards Soho – towards the flat above *The Venus Fly-Trap* – Valda told her husband about the exchange with Eddie Palmer. She told it sadly; without recrimination and, or so it seemed, as if accepting an inevitability.

'He's crazy,' growled Hodge.

'*He* doesn't think so.'

'Meaning *you* don't think so?'

'Crazy, maybe,' said Valda quietly. 'But crazy mad. Mad enough, I'd say. That was his sister we just watched being fed into the fire.'

'So?'

'He blames Peters.'

'Peters bought her a car from his winnings, that's all.'

'Not to Eddie.'

'She was lucky for him . . . it was a gesture.'

'Stop kidding yourself, Tommy. Men like Peters don't go for gestures.'

'What else?'

'Okay, kid yourself.' Valda's tone carried impatience. 'Just don't kid *me*.'

'What the hell . . .'

'Peters is scum. You know it. I know it. Who the hell are we conning? Young Eddie's mad and I don't blame him. In his shoes *I'd* be mad.'

The outburst silenced Hodge. He drove towards the centre of the capital in silence. Brooding. Scowling. Living with private thoughts which played havoc with his peace of mind.

Quite suddenly he muttered, 'Guns.'

'They're around,' said Valda.

'Y'mean . . .'

'No.' She shook her head. 'Not from me.'

'That's a relief.'

59

'Anyway, I wouldn't know where.'

'We run a respectable place,' growled Hodge.

'Think so?'

'Respectable,' repeated Hodge harshly.

'Yeah . . . a respectable clip-joint.'

'Hey, listen,' said Hodge angrily. 'Alongside some dumps *The Fly-Trap* is a monastery.'

'Sure,' agreed Valda. 'But for how long?'

The expression 'weighed down with sorrow'. Like so many clichés, it contains some truth. There is indeed a 'weight' to sorrow. Not the weight that can be measured in the pan of a balance; not a concrete weight; not a weight that can be handled or passed around. But a weight, nevertheless. An abstract weight. Like the weight of a sunbeam or the pressing-in weight of a confined space. Like the weight of darkness or the threatening weight of impending catastrophe.

Any man who disbelieves that genuine sorrow has its own weight is fortunate, or without feeling.

Certain it is that, in the living room of their very ordinary house in Poplar, the three members of the Palmer family knew all about sorrow's weight. It entered the room with them and became a part of the room. It brought with it a feeling of helplessness; as if life could no longer continue beneath its burden.

Having removed their outer clothes, each did something with which to busy the hands.

Freda Palmer murmured, 'I'll make some tea. I – I think we need it.'

Then she moved wearily into the kitchen, filled a kettle, turned a gas tap, struck a match . . .

Sidney Palmer lowered himself into an armchair, took a packet of cigarettes and a box of matches from a side-table, chose a cigarette, struck a match . . .

Eddie Palmer also lowered himself into an armchair, lifted the case from the carpet alongside the chair, removed his trumpet, fingered the valves . . .

It was as if each of them had an urge to touch something.

To handle some familiar object; some object which had not changed since the death of Daphne. Some gossamer link with the normality which had once been accepted as so ordinary. Some lifeline upon which to hang, rather than be drowned in the maelstrom of grief; rather than be squashed into nothingness by the weight of personal misery.

Freda carried a tray holding three beakers of strong, sweet tea from the kitchen. She set the tray on the hearthrug. Each in turn took a beaker, then Freda lowered herself on to the sofa. They sipped the tea in silence for a few minutes.

Then as if asking a simple question which required a simple answer, Freda Palmer murmured, 'Why?'

'Forget it, pet.' It was a stupid thing to say, but Sidney Palmer was in no state to make erudite remarks.

'*Forget* it?' Freda stared at her husband.

'No, I mean *leave* it,' Sidney corrected himself. 'Just – just leave it, pet. We all miss her. We all . . .'

'Peters.' Eddie dropped the name into the awkward conversation. He seemed to masticate the word, then spit it out, as if it was foul-tasting.

Sidney said, 'Look, Eddie. It won't do any good . . .'

'Peters. The mobs. That's "why".'

'Mobs?' Freda Palmer frowned at her son.

'The "firms",' rasped Eddie. 'The tatty bloody yobs who think they own all the muscle in the world. The . . .'

'Leave it, Eddie,' pleaded the elder man.

'No.' The woman watched her son. She said, 'What mobs?'

'It's all right, pet,' the elder man fought to protect his wife from the raging bitterness of his son. He said, 'It's all right. It's . . .'

'Yeah, it's "all right".' The hurt made the sarcasm jagged and ugly. 'I once had a kid sister, but it's "all right". A fink. A bastard. A louse not fit to breathe the same air, flashed the good-time under her nose. Turned her into a whore. Bought her a fancy motor car and let her kill herself in the damn thing. But it's "all right". You, pop, everything's "all right". The hell it's all right! It's all *wrong*. It's lousy. It's rotten. It stinks. Grab the truth, pop. Grab it. It burns – it

61

burns, down to the bone – but grab it and hold it. Your daughter – my sister – died because germs like Peters think they run the world and you say it's "all right". God Almighty, pop, what does it take to make you fight back?'

Eddie lowered his head after the outburst, as if the surge of passion had drained him of strength.

In a quiet voice Freda said, 'Mobs. You said something about mobs.'

'I don't know, ma.' The voice was heavy and not far from defeat. 'I don't know which mob. Which anything. Only Peters. And that Tommy Hodge hasn't the control he once had.'

'Mr Hodge?' Her son's talk was beyond the ken of the woman. She said, 'You mean . . .'

'Easy, pet.' Sidney Palmer tried to calm the emotional storm. 'We're guessing. Eddie could be wrong. We've no . . .'

'No!' The woman brushed her husband's attempt to quieten things aside. 'I want Eddie to tell me. I want to know. Mobs?'

Eddie sipped at the tea to moisten his lips. He shook his head, slowly, as if uncertain. As if bewildered.

He said, 'Ma, I don't know. Honest. I don't *know* . . . not for certain. Just a gut feeling. Rhodes. That animal, Peters. They're not customers. Every night? They're not *customers*. So, what the hell *are* they? That's all. That's all I'm really saying.'

In the flat above *The Venus Fly-Trap* Hodge was making a telephone call. Valda still wearing the dark dress she'd worn at the funeral service sat on a leather-covered ottoman, clasped her fingers in front of her closed knees, listened to the one-sided conversation and did little to hide her disgust.

Hodge was saying, 'Eddie. Eddie Palmer . . .

'Yeah. He leads the combo. His father's head waiter . . .

'Oh, sure . . .

'I know, but the Palmer kid . . .

'Yeah. The one who drove herself on to a slab the other day. She was Eddie's sister . . .

62

'Okay, but he's taking it stupid. Crazy talk about guns . . .
'Peters. Who else? . . .
'Yeah. He's angling around for a shooter and, if he gets it, he'll use it . . .
'Yeah. That's my guess. I thought you should know . . .
'Sure. I think he means it . . .
'Look, I run a good place here. I can't afford any shoot-outs between . . .'

Hodge glared at the telephone, then replaced the receiver on to its prongs.

He muttered, 'Damn creeps. He'll "fix things". What things? I don't want guns in my place. That's all. To warn the Peters creep to keep away for a while. That's all.'

'That's a new tune, lover boy,' said Valda sweetly.

'Eh?'

'New, y'know, but you sing it without heart.'

'What the hell . . .'

'You damn near sang *Rule Britannia*, when they rustled bank notes in your ear.'

'They offered a good price.' Hodge stood up, pushed his hands into the pockets of his trousers and frowned at his reflection in a bevelled mirror above the fireplace.

'For what?' purred Valda.

'Eh?'

'A good price . . . for what?'

'For this place.' Hodge pulled a hand from its pocket and waved it vaguely. 'For one of the best nighteries in town. For . . .'

'For what *was*.'

'For what still *is*. What the . . .'

'Shove it, lover boy.' Her voice was harsh. Brittle. She tilted her head and watched him mockingly. She said, 'I'm not new in from the sticks. I *know*. We made this place. Both of us . . . we *made* it. You sell it out to them and you dump it smack into a jungle. And you? You'll be the front man. That . . . and only that. They'll tell you which key to fart in. And the Palmer kid? The poor, dumb bitch we just watched burn? There'll be more Palmer kids than you can count.

63

More guns than *that*. It's their world, boy. Theirs . . . and they want you in it. They want this place in it. And if they *get* it?' She smiled tauntingly. 'Then, pick up a telephone and try burning somebody's ears off . . . they'll be round to nail *your* ears to the nearest door.'

Hendon. Strictly speaking not part of the capital, at the most a suburb on its north-west fringe. The home of a police college. The point where the A1 and the M1 fork, each to race north for the Midlands and farther.

Hendon boasts quite a few mini-mansions; multi-storeyed houses standing in their own grounds; enjoying the privacy of high walls or equally high and thick beech hedges. There is unpretentious wealth in Hendon. Real wealth, handled and enjoyed by men to whom wealth and power are the normalities of life.

One such man had a soft, croaking voice.

He allowed his fingers to rest on the telephone receiver he'd just returned to its place. A gentle sardonic smile played tag with his lips as he appreciated the puny stupidity of Hodge. A night-club-cum-gambling-house; one more Soho property which might, or might not, be worth his attention. A young woman, little more than a girl, a brainless little brat who presumably had had visions of high-life and glamour. Such little things. Such unimportant things.

And yet Hodge had sounded so agitated. So worried.

Assuming *The Venus Fly-Trap* was worthy of consideration, Hodge was a doubtful proposition, even as a manager.

The large man – the obvious 'minder' – who sprawled in an armchair in one corner of the beautifully furnished office said, 'Trouble?'

'Hardly that,' croaked the man. 'Hodge.'

'That cabbage.' The large man examined his manicured fingers. To him they were of far more importance than Hodge.

The man with the croaking voice moved his hand from the telephone to the intercom set which also shared the desk surface.

He pressed a toggle and rasped, 'Rhodes?'

A man's voice answered, 'He's waiting.'

'I'll see him.' He released the toggle.

The large man in the armchair made as if to push himself to his feet.

'No.' The man behind the desk waved him to remain seated.

The large man gave a quick understanding nod, then relaxed into his previous sprawl.

The door opened and Rhodes entered the room. He walked across the few yards of carpet between the door and the desk and there was about the way he moved a silent arrogance which amounted to near-contempt. Many men had walked those few yards of carpet. Some with fear. Others with trepidation which was not too far short of fear. Almost all with some degree of that awe reserved for the presence of despotic authority.

Rhodes was an exception.

The man with the croaking voice glanced at a chair positioned near the desk and said, 'Sit down.'

Rhodes sat down.

There was no preamble.

The man with the croaking voice said, 'Peters. Tell me.'

'What?'

'Don't be fancy, Rhodes. Just tell me.'

'What would you like to be told?' Rhodes smiled.

'Do you go for him?'

'Is that important?'

'I wouldn't ask.' The croaking man's eyes narrowed.

'Okay. I don't like him.'

'Why?'

'His mouth.'

'And?'

'His liquor. His fly-zip.'

'So?'

'I like a man who can control those things.'

'Peters can't?'

'You've seen,' said Rhodes.

'Yeah.' The man with the croaking voice paused, then added, 'I've seen. I've also just heard.'

'What?'

'Eddie Palmer.'

'The trumpet blower.'

'And Peters.'

'Peters smacked him around a little.'

'And other things,' said the man with the croaking voice.

'People get aggro-minded.' Rhodes smiled again.

The short-sentenced exchange was far more than a mere conversation. It was a little like verbal arm-wrestling; a test of strength, a quietly fought battle of personalities.

The man with the croaking voice said, 'Palmer's building up a vendetta.'

'Yeah?'

'You'll know why?'

'About his kid sister?'

'That's what it's about.'

'The trumpet blower has bottle,' observed Rhodes.

'An opinion.'

'*My* opinion.'

'Yeah?'

'Peters had better watch his back.'

The croaking man said, 'Palmer? Bottle enough to use a shooter?'

'I'd say.' Rhodes nodded.

'Okay.' The croaking man paused. watched Rhodes's face, then said, 'Let's say we don't need Peters.'

'Let's say that,' said Rhodes flatly.

'Maybe slip the word to the Palmer kid.'

'He might listen.'

'Any favours you'll go along with.'

'And *will* I?' asked Rhodes.

'Stay safe,' croaked the man.

'But – er – Good night Peters?'

'Not us.'

'Have we ever?'

The man croaked, 'We have a patsy. Okay?'

66

Rhodes nodded his understanding.

The man croaked, 'You're a handy man to have around, Rhodes.'

'I'm told.'

'You know your way without road maps.'

'I keep the wind from my face,' admitted Rhodes.

The man with the croaking voice nodded a dismissal and, without another word, Rhodes stood up from his chair and left the office. He didn't hurry. He sauntered – almost swaggered – he was supremely sure of himself.

The minder in the armchair growled, 'A smart-arse.'

'Ambitious,' corrected the man with the croaking voice. 'Very ambitious, therefore very dangerous.'

Monday, July 3rd

Another day, another week, another month.

The sad fact is that misery is a finite emotion. It was a discovery being made by the Palmer family. The death of Daphne Palmer had not stopped the spin of the world; not even the spin of their own limited little world. The realisation – the realisation that the loss no longer impinged itself upon the apparently less important business of living – brought on a feeling of guilt. And, like snow melting into slush, the guilt melted into anger. Anger with themselves that they could, in so short a time, adapt to the absence of a daughter and a sister. A more general anger directed against a world whose normality forced upon them the necessity to forget.

As head waiter Sidney Palmer could transform his anger into petty tyranny. The cutlery and crockery were never sparkling enough to discourage some testy remark. The table service was never smooth enough to satisfy him. The younger waiters muttered their complaints to each other in corners. The elder waiters frowned their concern, but for the moment retained their loyalty.

Joseph, the wine waiter, said, 'Sidney, it's not *their* fault.'

'I don't know what you're talking about.'

'I think you do.'

'They're sloppy.'

'If they're sloppy now, they were more sloppy before.'

'Before what?'

'Sidney, relax a little. For your own sake . . . relax.'

'I'm doing my job. Is that wrong?'

'The *way* you're doing it.'

'Do I tell you which wines to suggest?'

'No.' Joseph sighed. 'I'm sorry, my friend. I understand . . . the others, too, I hope.'

On the stand Eddie was equally dictatorial. Facing *The*

Opus – with his back to the diners – he could talk in a near-normal tone knowing that what he said would not be heard by the customers.

'For Christ's sake! We come in . . . *together*. Don't drift in, like a bunch of bloody amateurs.'

Steve muttered, 'Okay. Give us a direct lead-in and we'll be there alongside you.'

'The next time will be the first,' growled Eddie.

'Steady, boy,' warned Paul from the piano.

'Who the hell . . .'

'Right there!' Steve moved the slide as if to disassemble his trombone. 'I get paid to play. Not to take that brand of talk.'

'Hold it, Steve.' Paul's voice was both urgent and conciliatory. He said, 'Okay, Eddie. You're hitting rough water these days. Don't throw your friends overboard. That won't help.'

Eddie took a deep breath, then said, 'Okay . . . skip it. Let's try *After You've Gone*.'

There was even a reason for the choice of number. The third chorus was trumpet work; open horn; full blast. Eddie pointed his instrument directly at Table Twenty-Seven and blew as if he wanted to burst the eardrums of that table's occupants.

Petty things. Silly things. Things calculated to add to the hurt, rather than to help. But both Sidney and Eddie Palmer were human enough to want to spread their own hurt to others, in the mistaken belief that others could share it.

It was closing up to eleven o'clock. Eddie and *The Opus* had just taken over the stage from a coloured torch singer who'd tried, with very limited success, to belt out *If You Go Away*, Bassey-style; they were into the first chorus of *My Baby Just Cares For Me*. Hodge was 'circulating', stopping at tables and exchanging empty pleasantries with customers. Sidney Palmer was stationed at his usual corner, watching waiters and diners alike; sombre-faced and almost eager to find fault. Valda moved into the dining-cum-concert-room from

69

the gaming room. She stood in the shadow at one end of the bar and watched the man with the croaking voice enter the room with his two accompanying muscle-men and stand to survey the scene of the night's activity.

Rhodes caught the eye of the croaking man and lifted an enquiring brow. The croaking man moved his head in a barely perceptible shake and Rhodes returned his attention to Table Twenty-Seven.

The croaking man and his two companions stood, motion-less except for their eyes, for a few minutes then, at some unseen signal from the croaking man, one of the muscle-men walked quietly to the bar.

The barman said, 'Yes, sir?'

'This.' The muscle-man took a neatly wrapped package from his mac pocket and placed it on the bar counter. He rested his hand on the package as he said, 'Eddie Palmer.'

'Yes, sir,' said the barman politely.

'The kid fronting the band.'

'I know Eddie Palmer, sir.'

'Give him this.'

'Er, yes, sir.' The barman looked puzzled.

'Later. When the show's over.'

'Certainly, sir.'

The muscle-man removed his hand and the barman took the package.

'Just him,' warned the muscle-man.

'Yes, sir. I'll see to it.'

'Nobody else.'

'I understand, sir.'

While the muscle-man watched, the barman placed the package carefully on a shelf behind the bar.

'It's okay there?' growled the muscle-man.

'Quite safe, sir.'

'No nosy bastard gonna ask about it?'

'I assure you, sir.'

The muscle-man gave him a cold stare and said, 'You'd better be right, mac.'

The muscle-man returned to his position alongside the

70

croaking man and, for the space of about five more minutes, the trio stood watching the activity in the dining-cum-concert-room. Then they left.

Valda had watched the manoeuvre involving the croaking man, his two minders and the barman. She waited until the trio had left, deliberately waited another ten minutes to be quite sure, then made her way unobtrusively to the area behind the bar.

She exchanged a word here and there with the staff serving drinks and, eventually, reached her chosen destination. She stood with her back to the shelf and with the fingers of one hand touched the package, explored the outline, as well as she was able, then caught the eye of the barman who had taken possession of it.

She said, 'The packet?'

'It was given to me by a customer, ma'am.'

'A customer?'

'I – er – I took him to be a customer.' The barman looked worried.

'Okay.' Valda smiled. 'He was a customer . . . what else?'

'For Eddie?'

'Yeah. It would be.'

'Er – shouldn't I . . .'

'It's okay.' Once more Valda smiled. 'The – er – "customer" . . . he's *always* right.'

Tuesday, July 4th

It was almost three o'clock that morning when Joseph, the wine waiter, dropped Sidney Palmer off at his Poplar home. It had been a silent journey from *The Venus Fly-Trap* and after a grunted 'Good night' Sidney fitted his key into the lock and opened the front door.

He was (and he knew it) a man drained of energy; a man with only a spark of that necessary will to live without which life becomes little more than a heavy burden.

Daphne. The number of times he'd called her name in his mind. The number of times he'd retraced his whole life, almost hour by hour, in an attempt to find the flaw. He'd been wrong. Somewhere – somewhere in the past – he'd been *wrong*. All her life she'd been 'his'; Freda had been her mother – and a good mother; Eddie had been her brother – and no girl could have asked for a better brother – but granting all these things Daphne had been 'his'. Until little more than a year ago the bond had been so perfect. So absolute. 'His' Daphne. He loved his wife. he loved his son, but dammit he *worshipped* Daphne. From a child – from the moment he'd held her in his arms within hours of her birth – until she'd flowered into full womanhood. He'd watched. He'd marvelled . . . that an ordinary man like himself could grant life to such perfection. That had been the miracle. And having been allowed to perform that miracle, he'd accepted the responsibility.

And he'd failed. Somewhere along the line, he'd failed. He'd flawed the perfection. He'd done something he shouldn't have done. Or, conversely, he *hadn't* done something he *should* have done.

The realisation tormented him. It never left him.

He opened the living room door and like an automaton

72

walked to the armchair and touched his wife's forehead with his lips.

Freda, too . . .

Oh, yes. Freda, too. She no longer went to bed at a reasonable hour. Instead she sat alone, awaiting the arrival of her husband and son. Waiting and, no doubt, thinking. Remembering. Re-living the past in an abortive effort to understand the present.

Freda, too. But in her own way. Not like him, because he'd *never* struck her. *Never* bruised her precious face.

Freda said, 'Eddie?'

'He'll be along.' Sidney Palmer lowered himself into the second armchair. 'Half an hour . . . no more.'

'Tea?'

'No.' Palmer took out cigarettes and a lighter. 'We'll wait for Eddie.'

She nodded and relapsed into silence.

Palmer smoked for perhaps three minutes. then cleared his throat and said, 'We – we have to live, Freda.'

'I know.'

'With each other. That's what I mean.'

'Yes.' Her voice was dull and without feeling.

'You – er – you know how *I* feel.'

'I can guess.'

He hesitated, then said, 'You, too?'

'A tramp for a daughter,' she said softly. She spoke as if voicing secret thoughts; as if she was alone. 'That's how *I* feel.'

'For God's sake . . .'

'You asked.' The eyes suddenly blazed. The voice was heavy with bitterness and recrimination. 'That's how *I* feel. I loved her . . . of course I loved her. Anything. She could have had *anything*. But that wasn't enough. She turned filthy on us. We raised a whore. Both of us . . . *we raised a whore*.'

'No. I didn't . . .'

'Who the hell else?' Now the tone matched the eyes. 'All right. We have to live, but first we have to *talk*. I hit her.

73

The last time I saw her alive, I hit her. I hit her hard. I meant to hurt her. And I *did* hurt her.'

'It's not a thing to be proud of,' he breathed.

'No,' she agreed. 'Not a thing to be proud of, because it was too late. Years too late. I should have tanned her backside while she was still young enough to control.'

'Freda . . .'

'That's our mistake, Sidney. Don't let the sorrow blind you. That was the mistake we made. We taught *her* to hurt. To hurt us and get away with it. You? All right, you're her father. Were her father. But *me*? I should have known. I should have known better. I should have seen it happening. No, I *did* see it happening. A spoiled brat. And I didn't stop it. I didn't even *try* to stop it.'

Sidney Palmer leaned forward in his chair, stretched out a hand and clasped it over the hand of his wife.

'Freda,' he said softly. 'You were a good mother. You *were*. You still *are*. Fault, if there *was* fault, was with both of us.'

'No, no, no.' She shook her head sadly and refused to be comforted. 'The wrong things. So many times the wrong things, both of us.'

'All right, pet. The wrong things, but always for what we thought were the right reasons.'

'The *easy* reasons,' she sighed.

They sat there, silently sharing their sorrow; each trying unsuccessfully to comfort the other. But there was no comfort. In such circumstances there never is; what had once been said couldn't be unsaid; what had once been done, couldn't be undone; the clock and the calendar knew only one direction . . . and all the heart-searching, all the sorrow in the world, couldn't bring their daughter back to life.

They both heard the unmistakable throb of the Beetle's engine and Freda pulled her hand free, stood up from the armchair, and said, 'That's Eddie.'

Sidney Palmer leaned back in his chair. He stubbed out what remained of his cigarette into a nearby ashtray.

The misery stayed within him. The heartbreak remained.

Fine, perhaps his wife was right. Perhaps they *had* allowed her too much freedom. But today – as the twentieth century moved towards its close – what *was* too much freedom? And granting the right of all this freedom, freedom for what? To disobey, perhaps? The right to disregard all warnings given by anxious parents? The right for . . . everything? Even the right to be a whore? Even the right (God forbid) to *die* for that right?

Bitterness. Sadness. Helplessness. These and a score of lesser emotions churned his mind and made simple thought impossible. The resultant mix was something not too far removed from self-pity.

Eddie entered the room, but Sidney Palmer hardly noticed his son's arrival. Freda Palmer was in the kitchen, brewing tea and placing biscuits from their barrel onto a side-plate. Thus nobody saw Eddie place the gun and silencer on the table.

'There.' Eddie straightened and said, 'That's it, then.'

'What?' Sidney Palmer turned his head, jerked out of his reverie. and gasped, 'What the hell!'

Freda Palmer entered the living room carrying a tray. The cups and saucers on it rattled as she saw the gun.

She said, 'What on earth?'

'It's a gun,' said Eddie simply. 'A gun and a silencer.'

It was, indeed, a 'gun'. Specifically, a French-made **MAB,** *Le Militaire,* Model R, 9 mm Parabellum, semi-automatic pistol. The snout had been modified to take the three-inch-long, cylindrical silencer.

'Is it . . .?' Sidney Palmer swallowed. 'Is it loaded?'

'Yeah.' Eddie touched the chequered grip. 'An eight-shot magazine. And they're all in there.'

'Not in this house.' Freda Palmer placed the tray alongside the pistol. 'Get rid of it, Eddie. That's one thing we're *not* having in this house.'

'When I've used it,' said Eddie flatly.

'Eddie,' began Sidney Palmer, 'you're not going to . . .'

'Oh, yes,' interrupted Eddie.

'You're mad. Wherever you got it . . .'

75

'A friend. A present from a friend.'

'God help you, if you've friends like that,' said Freda.

'Valda fixed it. I asked. She fixed. It was as easy as that.'

Sidney Palmer almost groaned, 'Eddie. What do you want with a gun?'

'Okay.' There was soft but savage hatred in Eddie's voice. 'You asked. I'll tell you. For Peters. Who else? This damn family. We take things. We get pushed around like dirt . . . right? But not this time. Peters was hot on Daphne. Okay. Now, he's going to join her . . . on the wrong side of a crematorium curtain. Does *that* answer all the questions?'

'Get rid of it,' breathed Sidney Palmer.

'No way, pop.' Eddie's tone was as hard as his eyes. 'No bloody *way*.'

Like the rise of a curtain on a long-running show; the same feeling of constricted monotony; the same food to be prepared in the kitchen, the same dishes to be carried to the tables, the same wines to be suggested, the same click of counters in the gaming room, the same snap of the turned card, the same ivory tinkle of the ball as it danced into a slot in the roulette wheel.

The same bloody *everything*!

Eddie Palmer fingered the valves of his trumpet, eyed the scattering of early-evening customers, glanced at his watch to check that it needed another fifteen minutes before the opening triplets of *Opus One* marked the start of the stage show, then strolled around the perimeter of the dining-cum-concert-room.

It was a seven-day-a-week squirrel-cage. The treadmill graft of that fringe of show business few people even think about. Okay, *he* could vary it slightly. A new arrangement here. A new number there. But the hell, that was only like changing the colours in the limelights. It didn't really *alter* things. The same high-class lushes would still totter up to the stage and make the same stupid 'requests'. That damn film, *Casablanca*, had a lot to answer for. Sure it was a good film – one of the best – but the tune *As Time Goes By*. Christ, it was *every-*

76

body's hit number. That and maybe half a dozen others. Okay, but anything up to ten times each week! Why not buy a blasted record, stay at home and save money?

He almost collided with Valda Hodge.

She smiled and said, 'Watch it, boy. Come back to here and now.'

'Sorry.' He returned the smile, hesitated, then added, 'And thanks.'

'For what?'

'I got it last night.'

'You're playing riddles with me, kid.'

'The gun,' he said softly. 'What else?'

She took a deep breath then, equally softly, said, 'You've got yourself a gun?'

'Sure.' Eddie stared.

'You're laying eggs, kid,' she said flatly.

'I asked you to fix one and . . .'

'Not me, little boy.' The words were harsh and angry. 'I said "No". I *meant* "No". If you've found a shooter under your pillow, leave me strictly out of your calculations, kid. It didn't come from little Valda.'

'It came from somebody.'

'Okay. Now be wise. Lose the damn thing.'

'No way.'

'Hey.' The anger became an urgency. 'Listen to the wisdom of an old, old lady. Sling it. Bury it. Anything. But, for Christ's sake, don't *use* it.'

'On Peters.'

'Forget it, Eddie.' The urgency became a pleading.

'No way.'

'Look . . .' She floundered for words. 'You're – you're a little crazy. Y'know that? Crazy. You have loose marbles up there in your skull. Who knows? Christ . . . who *doesn't* know? You've shot your mouth off too much. This thing between you and Peters. Everybody knows. They'll . . .'

'You're forgetting.' Eddie seemed to freeze. The words were forced out from between lips which hardly seemed to move. 'I had a kid sister. Right? A nice kid . . . till Peters

77

moved in. Then she became *not* such a nice kid. You remember that? And he bought her a car. Right? He bought her a car and he let her drive the damn thing. And that was the last thing she did on this earth. And Peters knew. He *had* to know. The cops contacted him. Told him.' He paused, then continued. 'He was here that night. She was on a slab smashed to hell. But that bastard couldn't care less. He killed the poor little cow . . . and couldn't take time off to even *look*.' Again a pause. 'I don't hate easily, lady. But Peters . . . Okay, he knows. He knows how I feel. Maybe he even knows I have a gun. That, too, is okay. I'd like him to know. I'd like him to sweat a little. To wonder. To wonder just when. To *know* that one day soon I'm going to squeeze that trigger and blow the bastard clear off this earth.'

It was a little after ten o'clock. The stand-up comic was working his nuts off for laughs and getting nowhere. His timing was all to hell, and nobody wanted to hear blue jokes with whiskers round their chin.

Valda said, 'Pay him off. He's even making me blush.'

'He's engaged for the week,' muttered Tommy Hodge.

'Who the hell told him he was a comedian? Who the hell told *you* he was a comedian?'

'Bloody agencies!'

'Pay him off,' repeated Valda.

'Yeah.' Tommy Hodge nodded.

A waiter moved unobtrusively alongside Sidney Palmer and said, 'From the chef, Mr Palmer. We're running short on oysters. Everybody seems to have ordered oysters this evening. Any booked tables? Specific orders? The chef wants to know. please.'

Sidney Palmer turned, glanced at the open book on the shelf-desk behind him and said, 'No booked orders. Tell him. Use what he has left, then they're off the menu.'

'Yes, sir.'

At Table Twenty-Seven Peters rose to his feet and walked towards the swing-door with the word 'Toilets' above it.

From alongside the stage, Eddie Palmer walked around

78

the outside of the dining-cum-concert-room and made for the same door.

Beyond the door was a carpeted passage with, at the farthest end, a solidly built fire-door; a door with a panic-bar means of exit, but no means of entry. The Gents' toilet was on the left of the passage.

The toilet facilities were more than merely 'adequate'. On the right of the door was a black marble 'vanity shelf' below a tinted mirror and four hand basins complete with hot and cold water taps and soap dispensers. The 'stalls' were of matching black marble. The four W.C. alcoves had polished oak doors, as also had the narrow ceiling-high cupboard alongside the alcoves . . . the cupboard in which were kept brooms, squeegees and similar cleaning equipment.

The door opened and Peters entered the empty toilet. Almost as soon as the spring had closed the door, it opened again and Eddie Palmer entered.

'Cosy, eh?' murmured Eddie.

'Eh?' Peters turned to see who had spoken.

'Just the two of us.'

'You again, smart-arse?' Peters's mouth curled.

'I owe you things, Peters.' Eddie balanced himself on the balls of his feet.

'Yeah?'

'A beat-up . . . among other things.'

'Blow, kid.' Peters made a dismissive movement with one hand. 'You're getting to be a nuisance.'

'But only for so long . . . eh?' The impression was that Eddie was working himself up to a necessary point of action. His voice took on a snarling quality as he continued, 'As far as you're concerned only until . . .'

'Take off, punk. You've had one taste . . .'

Eddie literally threw himself at the other man. He grabbed for the lapels then, via the momentum, slammed Peters against the tiled wall. Peters's head cracked against the tiles and for a moment he was dazed. Long enough – just long enough – for Eddie to release the coat lapels, stand back and swing a bunched fist at the unprotected gut. Peters doubled over and Eddie drew back the same fist with the intention of hammering home an uppercut at the unprotected face.

The toilet door opened and Rhodes's voice said, 'Hold it, kid.'

Eddie glanced up and gasped, 'Keep out of this, Rhodes.'

'*Knock it off!*' There was hard authority in the words.

'This,' rasped Eddie, 'is a very private quarrel.'

'Not now, it isn't.' Rhodes grabbed Eddie's arm and, with ridiculous ease, twisted it high behind his back.

'The hell, Rhodes . . .' began Eddie.

'Hold the bastard,' panted Peters.

Rhodes snapped, 'You too, Peters. Back off.'

'You want I should let this . . .'

'I want,' warned Rhodes coldly, 'that you should remember that if you start anything *I* step into the act.'

'I'm gonna . . .'

'You're going to back off, creep, or else.'

There was a clash of wills. Not for long; not for more than about thirty seconds. Peters was wise in the lore of his chosen jungle; when tigers mouthed their displeasure, jackals moved beyond clawing distance. Scowling his reluctance, he straightened his clothes.

Rhodes gave Eddie's arm a warning twist and said, 'You too, kid.'

Eddie winced. then rubbed his released arm.

He said, 'You won't always be around, Rhodes.'

'True.' Rhodes grinned. 'Then – okay – open the man up and see what makes the wheels go round.'

'That'll be the day,' muttered Peters.

'You need to use this place, trumpet-player?' asked Rhodes.

'No.'

'Great. Don't let anybody keep you.'

Still rubbing his arm Eddie left the toilet.

'Punk,' muttered Peters.

'That,' said Rhodes, 'makes two of you.'

Rhodes moved to the stalls and unzipped his fly. Peters followed and took up a position at the next stall. As they urinated they talked. It was 'gangster' talk; underworld talk. The words had more than one meaning. Singly – even in groups – the words meant little, but their total added up to more than their sum.

Rhodes said, 'The kid has a shooter.'

'Yeah.' Peters concentrated upon emptying his bladder.

'You know that?'

'A whisper here. A whisper there.'

'He wants you on the wrong end.'

'And I'm gonna be there, that is for sure.'

'He's not the only one who wants you stiff.'

'I could name a few names,' admitted Peters.

'Peters. Listen good.'

'What?'

'Not the only one.'

'Uhuh.'

'Bear that in mind.'

'Who?'

'A guy.' Rhodes straightened his clothes and strolled to the row of washbasins. He added, 'A guy who could chew that kid up and spit him out.'

'Does the big man know?'

Peters joined Rhodes and. as they washed their hands, they watched each other's expression in the tinted mirror.

Slowly, deliberately Rhodes said, 'Yeah. The big man knows.'

'And?'

'He knows,' repeated Rhodes.

'So?' Peters angled for a more specific answer.

'Maybe,' said Rhodes, 'he ain't big enough.'

'Meaning?'

'Don't push things, Peters.' Rhodes pulled a paper towel from the wall container and began to dry his hands. He smiled and repeated, 'Don't push things. Be happy that I'm around . . . okay?'

81

Valda Hodge steered her Triumph Toledo east through the traffic of the city. She was, she knew, taking a risk; she was shoving a finger into a pie which, strictly speaking, wasn't even in her oven. She risked being burned . . . badly. There was an unwritten law; a very involved and carefully balanced law; a law which was enforced far more harshly and far more swiftly than the Law as understood by ordinary. run-of-the-mill citizens.

She braked suddenly as the scarlet bulk of a double-decker swung out from the kerb and forced its way into the flow of traffic.

Tommy . . .

Christ, Tommy would go hairless if he ever as much as *suspected. The Fly-Trap* was more than a club. More than an eating-house. More than a small gambling joint. As far as Tommy was concerned *The Fly-Trap* was just about everything. Twenty years back (thereabouts) he'd damn near put his soul in hock on the strength of a dream, and the dream had become a reality. And why? Because he'd worked and more than worked. He'd lowered his head and charged, full tilt, at a wall other people had called 'impossible'. And he'd battered a way through. The best and *his* . . . with no strings attached.

She turned the Toledo into Shadwell Highway and for the moment had a comparatively clear stretch of road ahead.

No strings attached . . .

But today? Could be the old boy was feeling his age. Could be he'd fought long enough. Could be the price offered was worth it.

Could be . . . Nuts!

In the business it was known as 'Hodge's *Fly-Trap*' and it was used as a yardstick. It was used as a measure of excellence. Bigger clubs . . . sure. And some of the bigger clubs, better clubs . . . sure. But size for size, nothing could come near it. And she knew her man. He wouldn't . . .

Easy girl. *Once upon a time,* he wouldn't.

But today?

She turned the Toledo off East India Dock Road and began checking street names as she passed.

The man with the croaking voice looked displeased. He sat behind the desk in his house in Hendon, stared at the seated Rhodes and allowed his fingers to fiddle with a gold-plated ballpoint. His eyes reflected his displeasure. They were cold and unblinking; slightly narrowed and peering at Rhodes's face, as if trying to penetrate the skin and read whatever messages were etched on Rhodes's mind.

Rhodes looked relaxed. There was a hint of mockery around his mouth. As if he found the croaking man's displeasure slightly amusing.

He said, 'I can't give you a warranty.'

'I said how I wanted it,' croaked the man.

'Last night,' drawled Rhodes. 'If the kid had had the gun I'd have been too late.'

'Don't be too late, Rhodes.'

'Now for instance?' mocked Rhodes.

'Not in *The Fly-Trap.*'

'He's gonna blow him away . . . somewhere.'

'I don't want it in *The Fly-Trap,*' repeated the man with the croaking voice. 'That brings the Law round. I don't want the Law.'

'You've worked a deal with Hodge?' asked Rhodes.

'If it's your business.'

Rhodes shrugged.

The man with the croaking voice said, 'I'm going to get the place.'

'Nice,' observed Rhodes.

'Hodge doesn't know it yet. But that's not important.'

Rhodes smiled.

83

The man with the croaking voice said, 'We were discussing Peters.'

'Yeah.'

'Peters and the Palmer kid.'

'It'll happen,' said Rhodes calmly.

'Outside someplace.'

'Where?'

'Who the hell cares?'

'I ride tight herd on him.' Rhodes suppressed a yawn.

'Not tight enough.'

'I can't be his damn shadow.'

'Yeah.' The man with the croaking voice nodded slowly. 'What?'

'Be his shadow, Rhodes. Just that.'

'And if he guesses?'

'Play it clever.' A smile touched the croaking man's lips. 'You're a clever man, Rhodes.'

'I don't have moss behind the ears,' agreed Rhodes.

'So, play it clever. Let the kid do the work, grab the gun, then play alibi games.'

'He gets away with it?' Rhodes sounded surprised.

'Why not?'

'We need a patsy.'

'We need nobody, Rhodes. The word is "undetected".'

'Could be.' Rhodes still sounded unconvinced.

'From Peters to Palmer. From Palmer to *The Fly-Trap*. A route I don't want the Law to follow . . . get it?'

'You're paying.' said Rhodes resignedly.

'Yeah.' The man with the croaking voice nodded. 'So, don't screw it . . . right?'

Valda Hodge pressed the bell-push. Timidly. As if half-hoping that nobody would answer; as if undecided whether or not she *wanted* somebody to answer.

Freda Palmer opened the door.

Valda moistened her lips and said, 'Mrs Palmer?'

'It's – er – Mrs Hodge, isn't it?'

'Yes.' Valda smiled. Her indecision disappeared. 'How did you know?'

'Sidney. You were at Daphne's funeral.'

'May I come in?'

'Of course.' Freda stood aside to allow Valda to pass. 'There – on the left, that's the living room.'

'Thanks.'

There was a chemistry there. A chemistry of immediate communication. It happens sometimes. Two people – strangers, comparative strangers – meet in given circumstances and, with little being said, they each know that they share the same wavelength. An instant 'friendship' is taken for granted.

As Freda closed the front door and followed her into the living room, Valda said, 'Sidney. I've left him doing his chores at *The Fly-Trap*. Eddie's busy working on a new number. I thought, perhaps, you and me . . .'

'Yes. I know. Please . . . sit down. I'll make some tea. Then we can talk.'

Tea. The English panacea; the universal medicine for all ills, for all ailments, for all problems. Tea and biscuits. Tea and scones. Tea and crumpets. But above all else . . . *tea*. In the rat-infested trenches of the Somme, in the blistering heat of the Western Desert, in the shelters of bomb-blasted London. Come Armageddon, the Englishman and the Englishwoman will no doubt await extermination quietly, calmly . . . sipping hot sweet tea.

Freda Palmer and Valda Hodge sat, sipped tea and talked as if they'd known each other all their lives. The subject of their mutual concern was Eddie.

Valda said, 'I'll have a word with him. Give him some hard facts . . . if you think it might do any good.'

'He's very strong-willed,' sighed Freda.

'Honey, he's a child,' said Valda sadly. 'And he's dealing with animals.'

'He – er – he has a gun,' volunteered Freda.

'I know.'

'Oh!'

'He asked me to get him one.'

'Y'mean *you* . . .'

'No, honey.' Valda shook her head. 'But I think I know who did.'

'Who?'

'I could be wrong. But that's not important. The question is . . . will he use it?'

'On Peters. If he gets a chance.'

'You think so?'

'I *know* he will.'

'He mustn't. You mustn't let . . .'

'You don't know my Eddie.'

'He *mustn't*.' What had been concern momentarily turned into an almost wild urgency. Valda continued. 'He's talked about it too much. His hatred of Peters. He's threatened too many times.'

In a dull voice Freda said, 'Peters killed his sister. That's the way Eddie looks at things.'

'So?' The urgency became touched with impatience. 'He shoots Peters. Nobody's likely to go bankrupt on wreaths, but your daughter's still as dead as ever she was. Peters is dead. Big deal! Your son's in prison till he's a middle-aged man. Does *that* solve anything? Does *that* make anybody happy?'

There was a silence. They drank tea. They mixed misery and sympathy in equal parts and exchanged the mix without needing to speak.

Then Freda muttered, 'They – they talk about mobs.'

'Yeah,' sighed Valda.

'Gangsters. Sidney and Eddie. They talk about men who . . .'

'Mrs Palmer,' cut in Valda.

'Freda, please.'

'Okay. Freda.' Valda paused, then went on, 'Woman-to-woman. We both have the same problem. Weak menfolk.'

'I – I don't know.'

'Yeah. Believe me.' Valda nodded. 'My man only needs one more nudge and he'll sell everything we've worked for to some rotten organisation. After that he won't have control of his own club.' Again she paused before continuing, 'Your man, Sidney – I'm sorry, Freda – but the truth is he crawls around, touching his forelock to people he should be spitting on.'

'Sidney's a good man.' said Freda.

'Sure he is. Too good to end up in the grinder . . . which is where they're *all* heading. Eddie? Eddie carries a hate inside him and, if he's let run wild, hate's going to ruin his whole life. Men!' She almost spat the word. 'Why the hell can't they see beyond their own stupid noses? Why do they have to have their hands held every minute of their lives?'

'Eddie loved his sister,' whispered Freda.

'Yeah . . . and Eddie has a gun.'

Freda said, 'I know. It's upstairs in one of his drawers.'

'Is it, by God?'

'I saw it today. I know. I shouldn't have looked, but . . .'

'But thank Christ you did, honey.'

'You mean you want to take it away?'

'No.' Valda chewed at her lower lip. 'He'd only get another. But, y'know, keep checking and when it isn't there, let me know.'

'Why? What are you . . .'

'I don't know.' Valda smiled at the elder woman. 'That's the truth, honey. There has to *be* an answer. Two women? We should be able to iron the kinks out between us.'

Freda Palmer took no comfort from Valda's encouragement. She stared at the dregs of tea in the bottom of her cup, and spoke as if to herself.

'No. There's no answer. No answer at all. I know. I can't put it into proper words . . . the way I feel. I mean. Since we lost Daphne. I've sat here. Alone. Just thinking. Wondering why. I mean . . . *why*? These – these mobs. These gangsters. I don't know who they are. I don't want to know. But I don't understand. I know they're violent, but why? And why should they have a monopoly in violence? Why that? What gives *them* the right? Eddie's been hurt. We've all been hurt. Ordinary people. Sidney. Eddie. Hurt . . . for no reason. We're not weak, we're just ordinary. And we've been hurt, badly. I'm – y'know – I'm not saying Daphne wasn't wayward. She was stupid. Her own fault, or perhaps my fault. But she didn't deserve . . . I mean, what happened to her. She didn't deserve *that*. So Eddie wants to . . . He wants to . . . He only wants to even things up a little. That's all. *Their* way. And why shouldn't he? Is that so wicked? These men. These gangsters people tell me about. *They* kill. They're *their* rules . . . aren't they? So I hope he gets away with it.' She raised her head and looked directly at Valda. She repeated, 'I hope he gets away with it. That's all.'

'Yeah, honey.' Valda nodded sad understanding. 'Me, too. But, y'know, I know damn well he won't.'

Had you asked around. Had you been inquisitive and questioned people who knew them. The answer would have always been the same. Tommy and Valda Hodge? A great pair. A perfect couple. Meant for each other.

Tommy? Okay, a little wild in his youth. A few times when he sailed pretty close to the wind of illegality, various things from blue movies to selling gold bricks. But nothing *really* bad. Nothing evil. Taking the suckers, nothing more harmful than that. And why the hell are suckers born, if not to be taken? And after fifteen years of marriage no two-timing, well, not *much* two-timing. Nothing an understanding wife couldn't overlook. Nothing blatant. Nothing Valda couldn't handle.

And Valda? Okay, a little brash, but most of that was a deliberate put-on. The old whore-with-a-heart-of-gold routine. It was her way and those who knew her understood. It went with the image. The nightclub image. The Tommy-Hodge's-wife image. It kept a lot of the would-be opposition at bay. Not all, but a lot. And those few who'd come close – those few who'd tried to ease a way between Valda and her man – carried scars to prove their failure.

Love? Sure there was love. Loads of the stuff. Not of the roses-round-the-door variety. But – and make no mistake – it was there all right. Tommy and Valda? Christ, they were *made* for each other.

All of which may have been true, but none of which prevented each of them hurling insults at each other, when the occasion demanded.

As, for example, that early evening as they dressed for their nightly stint as host and hostess at *The Venus Fly-Trap*.

'Take Rhodes,' snapped Valda.

'What about Rhodes?'

'*This* about Rhodes. Who the hell is he?'

'A customer.' Tommy struggled with his bow-tie. 'That's all you need to know. He's a customer.'

'Some customer!'

'What else? A good customer.'

'So now he's a *good* customer?' Valda settled her ample breasts into the cups of a brassiere.

'He's in every night.' Tommy yanked the silk and snarled. 'Damn this bloody tie.'

'Yeah, that's what I mean.'

'What?'

'Every night. We don't run *that* good a place.'

'What the steaming hell . . .'

'But him and Peters. Table Twenty-Seven. Every damn night.'

'Okay. *They* must think we're good.' Tommy started on his tie again.

Valda said, 'You're lying, boy.'

'Leave it.'

'Like hell I leave it.'

'Look, I don't want to . . .' Tommy dropped his arms. 'A favour, eh? Fix this tie for me.'

'Don't tempt me,' snapped Valda.

'Eh?'

'I might choke you. I might choke the lies back down your lousy throat.'

'Leave it,' shouted Tommy. 'Be grateful. Leave it.'

'Grateful?'

'Yeah . . . grateful.'

'Grateful for what?'

'That they come.' Tommy ripped the tie from his neck

89

and fumbled at the buttons of his shirt. 'The hell with it. I'll wear a silk polo.'

'The last of the big spenders,' said Valda sarcastically.

'I can't tie the damn thing. Why shouldn't I . . .'

'Rhodes and Peters. The one thing they don't do.'

'I don't want to know. I don't want to talk about it.'

'Okay. I'll do the talking.' Valda picked up a hairbrush from the kidney-shaped dressing-table and began to brush her hair. 'Rhodes and Peters. Every night. Money no object. *I'll* say. Peters had a run on the tables a while back. Since then – yeah and before that – peanuts. And they hate each other. Don't tell me you haven't noticed that.'

'Forget it.' Tommy tossed the shirt on to the bed.

'Like Siamese twins.' The brush fairly flashed across the surface of her hair. 'As close as that, but they hate each other.'

'Damnation. Will you forget it.'

'Since you ask . . . *no*!'

'Okay.' Tommy made an outward chopping movement with his hands. 'Okay, you're nosing around in some make-believe garbage can. But okay.' He dropped on to the edge of the bed. 'Say your piece, then zip it. Just don't take forever.'

'I don't like mysteries.' The brush-strokes became a little slower. 'Especially I don't like mysteries where bastards like those two are concerned. I want to know, Tommy.'

'Don't ask. honey.' It was a quietly-spoken plea.

'Tommy.' She dropped the hand holding the hairbrush to her side.

'Look . . .'

'No, *you* look.' The fizz had left the argument. Their talk was less animated. She pointed the brush at him accusingly and said, 'We're a good team, you and me. We've proved it. We can do things. We fit in. Or we *did* until the zombies moved in on the act.'

'The . . . zombies?'

'Yeah, the zombies. Specifically Rhodes and Peters. *Those* zombies. Now things are happening. Things that stink a little. I don't know what the hell's happening. I can make a good guess, and what I guess worries me. So I want to know, Tommy. I want to know before I'm old and grey. So, c'mon, give.'

'Once and once only,' said Tommy flatly.

'Okay. I don't need a plan-drawing.'

'The – er – the offer.' Tommy Hodge moistened his lips. 'Okay, we haven't agreed anything yet. But . . . y'know about the offer.'

'Get it out, lover boy,' she said grimly. 'Force yourself.'

'They're looking the place over. That's all.'

'That's *all*? What the hell . . .'

'Hold it, honey.' He tried to quieten her rising indignation. 'They have to keep an eye on their interests. It's their way. It's good business. They report back . . . see? Say things are running smoothly.'

'Rhodes and Peters?'

'Yeah.' He nodded.

'And?'

'And what?'

'If things *aren't* "running smoothly"?'

'I dunno. Maybe they'll . . .'

'*I* damn-well know.' The temper flared again and she wielded the hairbrush as if it was a weapon. 'They'll come visiting with axes and sledge-hammers.'

'Valda, that's . . .'

'So . . . they're giving the place the eye?' Her fury beat him into silence. 'Rhodes is watching Peters. Peters is watching Rhodes. Every bastard is watching every other bastard and everybody's watching *us*. Okay. So when the merry-go-round goes into reverse, who gets pitched out into the cold?'

'For God's sake . . .'

'*We* do, hubby darling. You and your little Valda. Right out there among the garbage cans.' She took a deep, shuddering breath, then continued, 'And for this we've worked our guts out. For this we've gambled our whole lives. My Christ, you talk about dumb-bells, I married the daddy of 'em all.'

91

As somebody once said, 'A week is a long time, in politics.' Very erudite, except it doesn't mean a damn thing. A week is a long time in so many things. From being buried up to the armpits in snow, to waiting for a revolution to burn itself out, from having the toothache to sitting on your rump doing sweet F.A. A week is *always* a long time.

It was long enough for Tommy and Valda Hodge to kiss and make up. It was long enough for Eddie Palmer to blanket his hatred a little; to concentrate a little more on his horn and a little less on his gun. It was even long enough for Sidney and Freda Palmer to start accepting the death of their daughter; long enough for the almost unbearable pain to ease itself into a near-nostalgic hurt they could learn to live with.

Indeed, had it not been for Peters, the chances are that the boat might have gradually stopped rocking, memories might have become blurred and people might not have been killed.

But as things happened a week was not long enough.

That Wednesday Peters poured himself a skinful. He was drunk . . . good and drunk. And whereas Peters sober was something of a nut case, Peters drunk was a raving maniac. Booze made him nasty; even nastier than usual. It gave him muscles he didn't own. It made him ten foot tall and four foot wide . . . and every ounce of him a louse.

Which, again, might not have meant much had not his flailing arms smacked into a tray of drinks a passing waiter was carrying and, when some of the drink from that tray spilled on to the dress of the whore he was trying to impress . . . Peters went berserk.

He left the launch pad with an explosion of bargee language directed at the waiter which could be heard well above the wailing of the singer who was spelling Eddie and *The Opus*. It froze the waiter in his tracks; it silenced the apology before it could be made and drained the colour from his face as he controlled a natural reaction to swing the tray and hit Peters across the mouth with its edge.

From across the table Rhodes murmured, 'Forget it, Peters.'

'The hell I forget it,' bawled Peters. 'This mother-sucking, dim, ham-fisted bastard . . .'

'Sweetheart. it doesn't matter.' The whore dived in in an attempt to calm things down. 'It won't stain. It . . .'

'And who the stinking Christ asked *you* to give an opinion?' raved Peters. 'I don't give a damn about your bloody dress. This stupid, dinner-suited dummy goes and throws . . .'

'Can I help, sir?' Sidney Palmer arrived at the table. He motioned with his eyes for the waiter to leave, then said. 'An accident, sir. I'm sure . . .'

'The hell it was an accident!'

'Sir, you're surely not suggesting . . .'

'Yeah. That's *just* what I'm suggesting.' Peters pushed himself upright, pointed a finger at the retreating waiter and shouted, 'I want that dim bastard fired.'

'I'm sorry, sir. But . . .'

'Don't be sorry, creep. Just bloody *do* it.'

'I assure you, sir . . .'

'Don't argue with me, punk. That dim bastard was waving his tray around like he didn't give a damn. Fire the sod.'

'I haven't the authority, sir,' said Sidney gently.

'No?' Peters glared. 'Then what the hell am I doing talking to the monkey when I want the organ-grinder?'

Hodge arrived at the table. Eddie Palmer was immediately behind him.

Hodge cleared his throat then said, 'I think you should leave, Mr Peters.'

'You think *what*?' For a moment it looked as if Peters was about to vault the table and fling himself at Hodge.

Hodge said, 'I'll arrange for a cab. Then you can . . .'

'Shove it!' Peters turned his fury upon Hodge. 'Shove your bloody cab. Shove your bloody club. You think you can sling me outa this crummy joint like I was a no-good . . .'

'The man said leave.' Eddie had edged himself closer to Peters. In cold rage his tone matched the loud-mouthed fury of Peters. He said, 'And the man gives orders here. So . . . leave.'

Again Peters turned and snarled, 'Who the hell asked *you* to . . .'

Peters had made a movement as if to go for Eddie.

Eddie whispered, 'Try it, friend. Just give me the excuse.'

'Eddie,' pleaded Sidney Palmer, 'this isn't your affair.'

'Any minute now it will be.' Eddie's eyes never left Peters's face. 'Any minute now, pop.'

'Eddie. Please!'

Peters pushed his chair aside and rasped, 'Lemme get at the two-bit, stinking little . . .'

'Leave, Peters.' Rhodes virtually 'appeared'. That expression fits . . . and that expression only. One second he was seated at the table. The next second he was between Peters and Eddie Palmer. The speed of his movement was almost unbelievably fast and smooth. He spoke in a cold, authoritative tone tinged with contempt. His mouth curled into a smile as he added. 'Quietly.'

'What the . . .'

'Or . . .' Rhodes's hand dipped into his jacket pocket. When he removed it the blade of the switch-knife flew open with on oiled click. He murmured, 'Cosmetic surgery could be arranged . . . on the house.'

Rhodes dominated the group. Everybody knew it – including Peters – and nobody even contemplated a challenge to that domination.

Hodge breathed, 'Get back to the stand, Eddie.'

Eddie hesitated.

Sidney Palmer said, 'Please, Eddie, it's over.'

'It's *not* over,' croaked Peters.

'No?' Rhodes's smile became more mocking.

Eddie left them and walked back towards the door leading to the rear of the stage.

Hodge said, 'Shall I – shall I call you a cab, Mr Peters?'

'Or an ambulance?' added Rhodes softly.

'One day . . .' whispered Peters.

'Yeah.' Rhodes nodded. 'You're going to get a little too tough. A little too frisky. Then you might need gelding.'

The words almost choked him as Peters said, 'I'll remember this, Rhodes.'

'Do that. Be wise. *Never* forget it.'

The still furious, but utterly subdued, Peters elbowed his way past Rhodes, past Hodge and Sidney Palmer and under the gaping stares of other customers reached the exit. As smoothly as he'd produced it Rhodes returned the switch-knife to his pocket then strolled towards the bar.

Hodge and Sidney Palmer busied themselves, quietening the fears of those who had been near enough to witness the incident.

Rhodes was into his first whisky-and-soda when Valda joined him at the bar. Behind them the hum of conversation was back to normal, forming a soft blanket of sound into which Eddie and *The Opus* stitched a pattern of small-group jazz.

Softly, almost sadly, Valda said, 'So? Now we *all* know.'

'Lots of people know lots of things, lady,' said Rhodes politely.

'Ain't that a fact?'

'What do I do now?' smiled Rhodes. 'Guess?'

'Guess?'

'At what we all know,' amplified Rhodes.

'Who the real boss is,' said Valda.

'Drinking?' asked Rhodes amiably.

Valda said, 'Lime, with a little gin in it. The barman knows.'

Rhodes raised a hand and without the order being given the barman mixed the drink and placed it in front of Valda.

They each sipped their drink, then Rhodes murmured, 'Your old man . . . who else?'

Valda frowned puzzlement.

'The boss,' explained Rhodes.

'Don't make me laugh.'

'Isn't he?'

'Like Peters. No.'

'Oh, *that*?' Rhodes chuckled, softly.

'Yeah . . . "that".'

'Peters was drunk.'

'Drunk or sober he doesn't even play in the same league.'

'He is,' drawled Rhodes, 'like other people. Tough with his mouth.'

'But you?'

'I'm not "people", lady,' said Rhodes, gently.

'True.'

'I'm *me*.'

They enjoyed drink-sipping silence for a few moments. They were – or so it seemed – quite at ease with each other. They talked a common language; a terse, quietly-spoken language; a language which contained its own brand of understatement.

With near-curiosity Valda asked, 'Would you?'

'What?'

'The knife?'

'What about the knife?'

'Would you have used it? Let's make it a hypothetical question.'

'Sure.' The smile was slow and friendly. 'A hypothetical answer. Too damn right. I would.'

'I wonder,' mused Valda teasingly.

'You need verification?'

'Maybe.'

'Ask Peters.'

Valda nodded as if convinced, then said, 'Eddie would have been very disappointed.'

'Eddie?'

'Eddie Palmer. The kid blowing trumpet.'

'That a fact?' Rhodes sounded mildly surprised.

Valda said, 'He thinks Peters is *his* meat.'

'Yeah?'

'For what he did to his kid sister.'

'I wouldn't know.'

'No?' There was gentle disbelief in the question.

'I don't run to kid sisters.'

'And now,' mocked Valda softly, 'you're being deliberately dumb.'

'Think so?'

'Prove me wrong,' she taunted.

'Okay.' Rhodes shrugged. 'If this Eddie kid has the nerve.'

'You think he hasn't?'

'Me? I don't know him.'

'You know him,' she countered. 'You know everything you *need* to know.'

'Okay.' Again he moved his shoulders. 'I think he's a young punk with a ball of hate curled up in his guts.'

'So?'

'So . . . he just might.'

'With a blade?' Valda seemed fascinated with the turn of the conversation.

'No.' Rhodes spoke slowly. Thoughtfully. 'Something a little less personal.'

'Less personal?'

'That's my guess.'

'A gun?' she asked quietly.

Rhodes grinned and said, 'What would I know about guns, lady?'

'What would you know about *anything*?'

'Yeah.' The grin broadened. He sipped his drink, then said, 'It's a wicked world. Guns. Knives. Blunt instruments. And all the tough bananas want a piece of the action.'

'Like Peters?'

'Yeah.' He nodded. 'Like Peters.'

'Like Eddie?'

'Like the kid. Like everybody.'

She smiled and said, 'But you on top?'

'Lady,' he murmured, 'every cake has to have its cherry . . . right?'

'Okay.' Her voice was soft but solemn. 'Let's talk about cakes. Let's talk about cherries . . .'

Thursday, July 13th

The man with the croaking voice was not happy at having been awakened by a telephone call in the small hours. He sounded trenchant. Annoyed at having had his sleep disturbed.

Rhodes fed coins into the slot, watched the occasional car pass the kiosk and allowed a sardonic smile to play tag with his lips. As always the man with the croaking voice wanted both the apple and the nut. Okay, maybe he got them both most times, but not from Rhodes.

The croaking voice rasped, 'So you backed him into a hole?'

'It wasn't difficult.'

'So why the hell ring me and tell me?'

'You wanted to know.'

'Eh?'

'You said "everything".' Rhodes tried to keep his voice suitably subservient.

'Sure. I'm not complaining, Rhodes.'

'That's nice.'

'Not there. Not at *The Fly-Trap*. You did the right thing.'

'Nice to know.'

'Okay. Now . . .'

'The Palmer kid wants his scalp,' interrupted Rhodes.

'That I know,' croaked the man. 'We've already decided.'

'So?'

'Put yourself in the clear, Rhodes. Be buddies again.'

'With Peters?'

'Look.' The croaking voice carried impatience. 'Everybody loves the creep except the Palmer kid. Follow?'

'Things don't happen that way.'

'*Make* them happen, Rhodes.'

'You're the man.' sighed Rhodes. He grinned to himself.

'Right. And keep him off the tiger spit.'

'That won't be easy.'

'Nothing's easy. I need sleep. It's not easy to get *that*.'

Rhodes's grin broadened. He said, 'My heart bleeds.'

'And don't get dumb.'

'Okay . . . I'm dumb.'

'Just keep me informed.'

'Sure. That, too. Even if it screws up your sleeping time.'

'Rhodes.' The croaking voice carried a threat. 'Don't get *too* smart-arse.'

Very gently – very deliberately – Rhodes said, 'Name some goon who could do without you.'

'Eh?' The impression was that the man with the croaking voice was suddenly very wide awake.

'Some guy who wants you blown away,' expanded Rhodes.

'You're saying things, friend,' croaked the voice.

'Not me,' said Rhodes innocently.

'Okay, tell me.'

'Peters.'

'Tell me about Peters, Rhodes. Don't get foxy.'

'He was stoned. He talked.'

'About what?'

'Propositions,' drawled Rhodes.

'What damn propositions?'

Rhodes said, 'He tried to proposition me. That's all.'

'Get specific, Rhodes.'

'Nobody,' said Rhodes amiably. 'gets specific along those lines. Not even a gink like Peters.'

'He was gassed,' said the man with the croaking voice.

'Even gassed.'

'Okay.' There was a slightly longer than necessary pause. 'What next?'

Rhodes said, 'Why don't *you* listen to the "specifics"? Saturday morning. When *The Fly-Trap* shuts shop. With a little nudging here and there it can be arranged . . .'

And at *The Venus Fly-Trap* – in the all-mod-con flat above

The Venus Fly-Trap – the re-run of the same old argument was being performed.

Tommy Hodge was already in bed. He relaxed between brushed-nylon sheets. The heavy silk pyjamas felt cool and comforting to his skin. The last cigarette of the day helped to quieten his nerves and he was almost happy as he periodically stretched out an arm to flick ash into the onyx ashtray on the bedside table.

That until Valda wandered in from the bathroom.

She was using a king-sized bath towel and tiny globulets of water still clung to the skin of her body where the bath towel had not yet done its work.

For a few moments Hodge viewed the body of his woman with professional approval. Okay, no longer young. No longer the slim, leggy female beloved of the soft-porn mags. But good. Very good. Rounded. Voluptuous. As sleek as a Derby winner and with nothing sagging. She knew how to hold herself. Knew that the middle years of a woman's life could, if she took a little trouble, combine real promise with real expertise. He'd picked a pip. He'd picked a bedmate capable of . . .

'And you're supposed to run this damn place,' snapped Valda.

'Eh?' Tommy Hodge's thoughts were jerked from the slightly naughty path along which they were meandering.

'A personal opinion.' Valda seemed to throw the words at her husband. 'Get some practice in on prayers. That's about the only card you still hold.'

'What the hell?' Tommy Hodge stared.

'Tonight.' Valda seesawed the towel across her shoulder blades. 'You are supposed to run this place.'

'Sure I run it.'

'Like tonight. Like the little balls-up with Peters.'

'I run it my way,' said Tommy Hodge heavily.

'Your way?'

'Yeah.' He nodded.

'With Rhodes.'

Hodge sighed. Women? The most perverse creatures in

101

creation. After a hard day a man has a tub, crawls into bed and wants to relax. He figures he's earned whatever corn might be coming his way. He sees his woman stripped and showing her wares. He thinks fine, this is what makes the world go round. This is one of the things life is all about. This is the meat inside the sandwich.

And what happens?

He sighed, 'Rhodes is a nothing. honey.'

'Don't feed the baby green apples.' She towelled her arms and the side of her body. She seemed to undulate in all the right places as the muscles moved beneath her skin. 'Peters was stewed up to the eyeballs.'

'So? What's with Peters'

'Without Rhodes he'd have run wild.'

'I can handle drunks.'

'The hell you could handle *that* drunk.'

'Drop the subject, sweetheart,' he pleaded.

Instead she said, 'And what about Eddie?'

'Eddie,' he murmured, 'is getting to be a pain. *That* about Eddie . . . since you ask.'

She began to towel her legs. Those shapely, rounded, highly sheened legs. From the ankle all the way to the crotch. That towel was having a whale of a time . . . a better time than *he* was having.

He flicked ash into the tray and added, 'Eddie poked his damn nose in. He'd no cause to . . .'

'You should be glad he didn't poke his *gun* in.'

'What gun?'

Tommy Hodge was becoming irritated by the conversation. Irritated and shocked. Guns . . . for Christ's sake. The hell, there she stood, having dried herself, with the towel draped around the back of her neck. doing nothing at all to help matters as far as *he* was concerned. Yapping on about guns and young kids who play trumpets and anything and everything other than the one thing she *should* be concentrating on.

He squashed out the cigarette and growled, 'Okay, let's

get this stupid argument out of the way then we can concentrate upon more important things.'

'Get that randy look out of your eye, mister,' she warned.

'I'm asking you . . . *what* gun?'

'Something else Rhodes knows. But not you.'

'Look, if the young idiot's . . .'

'Holy cow!' She let her temper fly. 'You who "run" this damn place. The big man. The guy who at this moment wants to demonstrate just how big he can get.'

'Hell's bells, honey . . .'

'The whole damn world and the vicar's cat knows. But not *you*. Eddie Palmer is about to put Peters where the crows can't touch him. Like you, he's itching to get started. And don't ever think he won't. He has what he wants. He has a gun. He has the bullets. He even has the guts . . . which makes a pleasant change around here. Lemme tell you, as far as Eddie Palmer is concerned Peters is already breathing air he is not entitled to. Tonight could have been the night. Tonight! It wasn't. And why? Because Eddie Palmer isn't that sort of killer. Oh, yes, he'll kill. Something else *you* don't know, big man. But he'll kill. Not like Rhodes. Not like Peters. He hasn't that brand of instinct. But he'll squeeze that trigger one day. A very special day. Not too far different from today. And you – the guy who "runs" things – will stand there and watch it. This personal boil-up. This one-time-too-many that'll be the blue touch-paper. And then . . .'

'And then,' growled Hodge, 'we'll have trouble.'

'No. Then a very nice kid will be put away because he stepped on vermin.'

'Yeah . . . trouble.'

Like a mist before a breeze her anger seemed to clear. It was replaced by something much deeper. More sorrowful. A strange, nostalgic remembrance.

She said, 'I sometimes wonder.'

'What?'

'Where the hell the man I married disappeared to. The man who'd have out-faced any mobster soiling the carpet with

103

his fancy shoes. Where? Where the hell did he go? Who castrated him?'

Meanwhile, Eddie Palmer sat in the privacy of his room; sat, already in pyjamas, on the edge of his bed. He sat, weighed a semi-automatic pistol in his right hand and wondered that such a comparatively small conception of high-class steel and superb workmanship could – or even *should* – result in such a perfect killing tool.

It was the first gun he'd handled in his life. It was surprisingly compact, but at the same time surprisingly heavy. Heavy not so much in weight as in solidity. It was a mass of internal moving parts – it *had* to be – and yet, however he handled it, there was no sound. No 'rattle'; nothing to suggest that it wasn't a single piece of metal. The fitting together of all those parts . . . God, it must be fantastically accurate. Take a trumpet. A trumpet – a good trumpet – was an example of superb craftsmanship. Dammit, a trumpet was a musical instrument and, like every other musical instrument, it was turned and fashioned to an almost impossible degree of accuracy. But shake a trumpet – shake even the *best* of trumpets – and tiny oiled movements could be felt (even heard) as the valves and pistons compressed the springs and as the springs responded. Okay, the same with this gun. It, too, had pistons, valves, springs – that or their counterpart – as complicated (maybe even more complicated) somewhere tucked away in its innards. But shake it – shake it as much as you like – not a sound. *Nothing.*

He held the pistol nearer to the bedside light to read the markings.

Along the blued-steel barrel it read *Pistolet Automatique MAB Brevete.* Then beneath these words, *Modele R Cal. 380.P.* Within a lozenge on the chequered grip were the letters MAB.

It was, he supposed, a French weapon. The spelling of the various words gave the clue. It looked a very *efficient* weapon and (because he'd counted them on the day he'd received the gun) he knew the magazine held eight rounds of ammunition. Eight shots. Eight squeezes of the trigger.

He lifted the silencer from the bedside table and screwed it on to the snout of the pistol. Again such a smooth but perfect fit. At a guess (and he was only guessing – he knew almost nothing about firearms), but at the guess the muzzle had been machined to take the silencer. If so the machining, too, was a work of art.

Christ!

The question was . . .

The question. A few hours back there'd have been one answer. Just that one answer. Had he had the gun *then*. No sweat, no problem, no qualms. Peters would already be stiffening.

Okay, but in cold blood? Deliberately? Without the taunts, without the egging on? In effect without Peters's own help?

Bloody funny, that. (He smiled wryly as the thought entered his mind.) In order to make sure of his own execution Peters himself had to help. Otherwise . . . there was one hell of a question mark.

Point the gun? Sure. Scare the living daylights out of the louse? With pleasure. But squeeze the trigger?

That needed something extra. Something he had to be given. Something only Peters could give him.

So Eddie Palmer stared at the pistol and sighed. Sure as hell he wasn't going to lug a damn gun around in his pocket just on the off chance. Equally – sure as hell – Peters wasn't going to oblige by visiting his bedroom just for the sake of exchanging insults.

'So,' he murmured. 'Balls. That's all. I'm playing one-man Silly Buggers.'

He unscrewed the silencer, placed gun and silencer back in their drawer, swung his feet from the carpet, wriggled himself between the sheets and switched off the bedside light.

The Day of Saint Swithin. The day when those ruled by the lore of the weather awaken, look through their windows and foretell the weather for the next forty days and forty nights. Confidently but erroneously.

And already it was raining.

The night rain of summer; the warm, soaking drizzle beloved of farmers and gardeners; the rain which soaks into thirsty soil to fatten crops and swell the coming harvest; the rain which in the city gives every street lamp its own halo, glistens the pavements and turns tarmac surfaces into black mirrors.

It was Saint Swithin's Day. The day for the rain. The day for the killing.

1.50 a.m.

Rhodes excused himself and left Table Twenty-Seven. He strolled with deceptive speed towards the swing-door with the word 'Toilets' above it. Down the carpeted passage. Past the Gents' toilet with the card bearing the words 'Out of Order' hanging on its knob. To the firedoor, closed and fastened by the panic-bar.

He eased the panic-bar from its central housing and opened the door.

The man with the croaking voice entered.

The duo of bodyguards made as if to enter, but Rhodes said, 'Just the one. We can't hide an army.'

The man with the croaking voice hesitated, then nodded, and the two muscle-men stepped back into the shadows. One of them raised the collar of his mac against the rain.

Rhodes re-engaged the panic-bar, led the way to the Gents'
toilet and, ignoring the card on the knob, entered.

'Where?' asked the man with the croaking voice.

Rhodes nodded towards the ceiling-high broom cupboard.
'There. He'll check the bogs.'

'But not there?' The croaking man was as suspicious as a
startled cat.

'I have a key. I'll lock it.'

'That makes me very vulnerable, Rhodes.'

'Your decision.' Rhodes shrugged. 'Nobody's after my
throne.'

'The two boys are outside, remember that.'

'Sure.'

'They'll be listening.'

'Uhuh.' Rhodes nodded.

'I don't trust people,' said the croaking man.

'Nor I.'

'I don't even trust *you*.'

'We can,' said Rhodes, calmly. 'call the whole session off.
Nothing easier. Go back to your nursemaids. I meet Peters
in here at two, as arranged. We talk. Maybe he says something. Maybe he doesn't. Maybe I understand. Maybe I don't.
Maybe I tell you everything he says. Maybe I tell you what
I want you to know. On the other hand . . .' Rhodes glanced
at the broom cupboard. 'One way you'll be sure.'

'All cosy,' sneered the man with the croaking voice.

'I should worry.' Rhodes smiled. 'If there's a hot seat I'm
not in it.'

'Okay.' The man with the croaking voice reached a decision. 'But don't cross me, Rhodes. Just don't cross me.'

'Would I?' murmured Rhodes.

The croaking man didn't answer. He stepped into the
broom cupboard. Rhodes closed then locked the cupboard
door. He slipped the key into his pocket and walked from
the toilet, down the carpeted passage, into the dining-cum-
concert-room and back to Table Twenty-Seven.

1.55 a.m.

On stage Eddie Palmer and *The Opus* lashed into the final, all-in chorus of *Sweet Georgia Brown*; the last chorus of the last number . . . which meant they could have the usual, tightly organised ball in order to leave the customers applauding for more. Ready to come back another night for more.

In the carpeted passage the killer ignored the notice hanging on the knob, opened the door, eased into the Gents' toilet, then closed the door. In the distance the sound of *Sweet Georgia Brown* pushed its way through the walls and could be heard quite plainly.

The killer wore gloves. Black leather gloves. tight enough not to be awkward, but well-fitting enough to give easy finger movement. The killer carried a blued-steel French-made MAB, 9 mm, semi-automatic pistol, fitted with a three-inch-long cylindrical silencer.

At Table Twenty-Seven Peters raised a questioning eyebrow at Rhodes.

Rhodes lighted a cigarette and murmured, 'No rush, pal. All the rest of our lives, eh?'

'Sure.' Peters nodded.

His smile was strained and not without a shadow of fear.

1.57 a.m.

On stage Eddie Palmer acknowledged the applause. He grinned happily at the audience, then stepped closer to the mike.

He said, 'Thanks for listening, folks. This is Eddie Palmer and *The Opus* wishing you a safe journey home and sweet dreams.'

He raised his trumpet to his lips, tapped out the four-beat tempo with his right heel and led the combo into the explosive opening bars of *Opus One*.

In the Gents' toilet the killer held the pistol in a double-handed grip. Pointed it at the closed broom-cupboard door and curled a finger around the trigger. As the crash of the triplet-opening two bars of *Opus One* carried from the dining-cum-concert-room. the killer squeezed the trigger, almost it seemed in tempo, and the pistol made a series of dry coughing sounds as it spat all eight rounds in an irregular pattern through the woodwork of the cupboard door.

In the dining-cum-concert-room Sidney Palmer strolled towards the swing-door with the word 'Toilets' above it.

Rhodes noticed the direction being taken by Sidney Palmer. For a moment he frowned, then the frown cleared.

1.59 a.m.

The killer's gloved hand trembled slightly as it carefully placed the empty pistol on the black marble 'vanity shelf' below the tinted mirror alongside the hand-basin near the door.

The killer opened the door, entered the carpeted passage, closed the door, then removed the 'Out of Order' notice from the knob.

In the dining-cum-concert-room Sidney Palmer paused for a moment to speak to a customer before continuing on towards the swing-door with the words 'Toilets' above it.

Rhodes said, 'Move naturally, Peters.'

'Sure.'

'Take your time . . . I'll follow.'

2.01 a.m.

Sidney Palmer pushed open the door of the Gents' toilet. The first thing he saw was the pistol. He stared at it for a moment recognised it, then picked it up . . . to be certain.

Peters reached the swing-door with the words 'Toilets' above it.

Sidney Palmer saw the bullet-punctured door. Saw the trickle of scarlet already creeping its way under the door.

Still carrying the pistol he returned to the carpeted passage.

Peters entered the carpeted passage from the dining-cum-concert-room end. He saw Sidney Palmer, saw the gun, and gasped, 'What the hell!'

Sidney Palmer moved his head as if seeking a way of escape then, as if in defeat, dropped his arm to his side and waited for Peters to raise the alarm.

Monday, October 30th

The three-day trial of Sidney Palmer was one of those things no police force ever wishes upon itself. The evidence (for want of a better word) could prove only two things. That a known mobster had been shot to death through the door of a locked broom cupboard. That Sidney Palmer had been found carrying the murder weapon within minutes – virtually minutes – of the known time of death.

Had he talked – had he offered any sort of explanation prior to the trial – the chances are Palmer wouldn't even have been charged. But instead – and for reasons he kept to himself – he was as dumb as a post. Polite, but rock-firm. He was innocent, and he had supreme faith in British justice. He refused to even open up to his solicitor until after the committal. After that he itemised things carefully, if not fully.

His plea was 'Not Guilty' and that was still his plea when he stood in the dock at the Old Bailey.

The Q.C. for the Prosecution did his best. He built bricks without too much straw. He did more than that; his skill was such that, as far as the examination-in-chief was concerned, those bricks had the outward appearance of re-inforced concrete blocks.

Unfortunately they crumbled under the cross-examination of the defending barrister.

'This gun, officer. The murder weapon. Can you tell the court whether it was examined for fingerprints?'

'Yes, sir. It was.'

'Are we to hear expert evidence along those lines?'

'Er – no, sir.'

'Why not?'

'They were smudged, sir.'

'Smudged?'

111

'Indistinct.'

'Not those of the accused? Is that what you mean?'

'We – er – we don't know, sir. We can only guess.'

'Guess?'

'Yes. sir, they *might* be.'

'Might,'

'Yes, sir.'

'But also might *not*?'

'We – er – we think they were.'

'Ah! I see you're resting your hands on the surround of the witness box.'

'Yes, sir.'

'Probably leaving fingerprints. *Your* fingerprints?

'It's possible, sir.'

'Therefore, working on the same proposition – the proposition that the accused *might* have handled the murder weapon – a stranger might assume . . .'

'Pardon me, sir.' The witness stepped into the carefully worded trap. 'We *know* he handled the murder weapon.'

'Ah, yes.' The defending barrister smiled mock-apology. 'We also *know* – the court knows – that *you* have stood in that witness box. What I'm getting at is this. On that same assumption – that same proposition – a stranger might equally "guess" that *you* have been a witness for the Defence?'

'I'm sorry, sir. I don't follow.'

'Your fingerprints on the witness box surround?'

'Yes, sir.'

'What does it prove?'

'That – that I've given evidence, sir.'

'Oh, no. That you *might* have given evidence . . . surely?

'Yes, sir.'

'That it *might* have been evidence for the Prosecution? Or equally that you *might* have given evidence for the Defence? Or again that you *might* merely have stepped into the witness box . . . for no good reason at all?'

'Yes, sir. I suppose so, sir.'

'In short it means nothing? It proves nothing? Even were your fingerprints identifiable, that fact of itself would be a

112

mere flippancy? Were they *not* identifiable the doubt raised would be far from "reasonable". It would be monumental?'

'I – er – I suppose so.'

'You only *suppose* so?'

'Yes, sir.'

'Yes, sir . . . what?'

'The doubt would be there, sir.'

'A monumental doubt?'

'Yes, sir, a monumental doubt.'

'As with the accused. Surely?'

'Well, sir, it's not quite . . .'

'That he handled the murder weapon? As you are handling the witness box surround?'

'Yes, sir.'

'No identifiable fingerprints?'

'None, sir.'

'Proving precisely nothing?'

'Proving nothing, sir. But . . .'

'No further questions, officer. Thank you.'

Much was made of the fact that Sidney Palmer had not professed his innocence; that, despite hours of interrogation, he had refused any form of co-operation with the police. Much was made of this by the Prosecution. It was argued – argued well and argued strongly – that an innocent man takes the first and indeed every opportunity to profess and underline his innocence. The Q.C. for the Prosecution emphasised this supposed irrefutable argument in at least half a dozen different ways. It was, when all was said and done, the keystone of the case.

The Defence Q.C. was almost grinning as he rose to his feet to cross-examine.

'Inspector, you were present throughout the questioning of the accused?'

'I was.'

'Never once was he questioned without *you* being there?'

'Not once, sir.'

'Indeed, as I understand it, you personally did most of the questioning?'

113

'That's correct.'

'How many hours of questioning, inspector?'

'I'll – er – I'll need to check the file, sir.'

'Approximately? I'll accept your approximation.'

'About fourteen hours. No more than sixteen.'

'Not all one session, of course?'

'Oh no, sir. Not one long session.'

'How many sessions?'

'Er – five. No, I'm sorry, six.'

'Six sessions?'

'Yes, sir.'

'Spread over how many days?'

'Until he was committed to this court.'

'And that period?'

'Five weeks, sir. Approximately.'

'Five weeks?'

'Yes, sir.'

'Six separate instances during which the accused was questioned?'

'Yes, sir.'

'Over a period of five weeks?'

'Yes, sir.'

'And before each session – before you resumed the questioning – did you administer the Official Caution?'

'Oh yes, sir.'

'You're quite sure?'

'Every time.'

'You know the wording of the Official Caution of course?'

'Of course.'

'For the benefit of the jury, inspector.'

'Sir?'

'The wording – the precise wording – of the Official Caution.'

'Certainly, sir. "You're not obliged to say anything, unless you wish to do so. But whatever you say ..." '

'That's far enough, inspector.'

'Sir?'

'You gave that caution six times?'

114

'I did.'

'Six times?'

'Six times, sir. Every time he was interviewed. Every time he was questioned.'

'You see, inspector, this puzzles me.'

'Sir?'

'In your examination-in-chief. By implication, if not openly, you conveyed the impression that the accused's silence – his refusal to give any explanation, any information concerning *why* he was holding the murder weapon – was tantamount to an admission of guilt. That in effect was *one* reason – a very important reason – why he's in the dock today.'

'Well, sir, if he was innocent . . .'

'He's innocent, inspector.'

'Sir?'

'Innocent. At this moment he's innocent. No more guilty than you or I. He only becomes guilty when – and if – the ladies and gentlemen who make up the jury decide that he *is* guilty.'

'Yes, sir. I'm sorry, sir.'

'You only *think* he's guilty.'

'I'm sorry, sir.'

'And what *you* think is of no importance.'

'I'm – er – sorry, sir.'

'When you charged him with this crime you also *thought* he was guilty.'

'Well . . . yes, sir. Otherwise . . .'

'Otherwise you wouldn't have charged him?'

'Just so, sir.'

'And as I see it that conclusion was, in the main, based upon his silence.'

'Er – in part, sir.'

'In part?'

'Yes, sir.'

'But, y'see, six times – each time you questioned him – you told him *not* to say anything.'

'Sir?'

'The Official Caution. You are *not* obliged to say anything.'

'Yes, sir.'

'A warning?'

'Well, sir, I wouldn't call it a . . .'

'If not a warning what else?'

'The – the law requires . . .'

'That you administer a caution?'

'Yes, sir.'

'A caution in the shape of an official warning?'

'I – er – I suppose so.'

'A warning to remain silent?'

'No, sir. Not exactly. More of a . . .'

'Very well, inspector. We'll split hairs. Advice. Advice that he *may* remain silent?'

'Yes, sir.'

'But – correct me if I'm wrong – not a word, not a suggestion, that if he accepts that warning his silence will be construed as an admission of guilt.'

'No, sir. It's not meant to be . . .'

'Is it meant to be a tacit admission of guilt, inspector?'

'No, sir.'

'Do the police – as opposed to a court of law – construe it as an admission of guilt?'

'No, sir.'

'For the benefit of this court, then. It's true to say that the accused was innocent at the time of his arrest?'

'Er – well, yes, sir.'

'He was innocent throughout fourteen hours of questioning?'

'Yes, sir.'

'When he was duly charged he was *still* innocent?'

'Yes, sir.'

'At the lower court . . . still innocent?'

'Yes, sir.'

'Today. Now. At this very moment. *Still* innocent?'

'Yes, sir.'

116

'And the fact that he has exercised his right of silence makes not one jot of difference. *He's still innocent?*'

'Er . . . yes, sir.'

'Thank you, inspector. By the way, was the accused photographed while in police custody?'

'Yes, sir. We have the right . . .'

'Quite. Photographed *and* fingerprinted?'

'Yes, sir. He was fingerprinted.'

'And what is known as the "paraffin wax test"?'

'Yes, sir. He agreed to be subjected to that test.'

'And the result?'

'Negative.'

'Both hands?'

'Both hands, sir.'

'Now correct me if I'm wrong, inspector. This test – this "paraffin wax test" – is one way of showing that a person has fired a handgun very recently?'

'A positive result shows that a man's fired a gun recently.'

'Always?'

'Yes, sir. Within a certain time scale always.'

'And a negative result?'

'It – er – it usually means he *hasn't* fired a gun. Within that time scale.'

'Usually?'

'Far more often than not.'

'But not always?'

'No, sir. Not always.'

'The result as far as the accused was concerned was negative.'

'Yes, sir.'

'I'm sorry. inspector. I didn't quite catch that answer.'

'The test showed a negative result, sir.'

'In other words, he *hadn't* fired a gun?'

'There's no absolute certainty with a negative result, sir.'

'But there's a possibility?'

'Yes, sir, a possibility.'

'A probability?'

'Er – yes, sir, even a probability. But no certainty.'

117

'A *good* probability?'

'A *fairly* good probability.'

'But – in all fairness – more than, say, a reasonable probability?'

'Oh yes, sir. More than a reasonable probability.'

'I ask that question, inspector, because at the end of this trial the jury will be asked to concern themselves with "reasonable doubt". "Reasonable doubt". "Reasonable probability". The two terms are interchangeable. wouldn't you agree?'

'I – I suppose so, sir.'

'Therefore, *more* than "reasonable probability" equates with *more* than "reasonable doubt"?'

'Er . . . yes, sir.'

'Thank you, inspector. I'm obliged. You've been very honest.'

The witnesses for the Defence took up much of the second day of the trial. They numbered five; Sidney Palmer himself and the four customers who had occupied the table at which he had paused on his way to the toilet. Palmer insisted that Peters shouldn't be called upon as a Defence witness; indeed he threatened refusal to take the stand himself if Peters was called to give evidence.

It mattered little. The defending barrister had already cracked the case for the Prosecution. Palmer's own evidence on oath, plus the corroboration of four independent witnesses, merely made doubly sure of a verdict which was already as certain as any jury's findings ever can be.

Palmer told a plain, unvarnished story. Of entering the toilet; of seeing the pistol; of picking up the pistol; of seeing the bullet-shattered door and the trickle of blood; of immediately returning to the carpeted passage. No, he didn't know the dead man; he'd seen him a few times in the dining-cum-concert-room of *The Venus Fly-Trap,* but he didn't know his name. He hadn't been a customer. Motive? How could a man have a motive for killing somebody he didn't even know? The key to the locked broom cupboard? No, he didn't have such a key; the orbit of his real authority began and ended with the waiting staff; the cleaning staff were only under his supervision while they worked in the dining-cum-concert room; his authority touched the fringe of the kitchen staff, but only in so far as there had to be some degree of liaison between the kitchen and the customers. The broom cupboard? Certainly he knew about the broom cupboard; everybody employed at *The Venus Fly-Trap* knew about the broom cupboard; equally, many of the customers must also have known about the broom cupboard. The key to the broom cupboard? He didn't know *who* kept the key to the broom cupboard; what he *did* know – from personal observation – was that the lock was a very ordinary lock, the sort of lock likely to work with most keys of the correct size. His 'working dress'? That was something Mr Hodge was very keen about; he wore full evening dress; white tie and tails; tailored to fit as perfectly as possible; it was his habit to keep all pockets empty in order not to spoil the 'hang' of the suit, and certain it was that anything as large and as bulky as the murder weapon – plus the silencer – would have caused a most unsightly bulge, which *must* have been noticed.

The four diners with whom Palmer had exchanged pleasantries on his way to the toilets were adamant and impervious to cross-examination.

His demeanour? Definitely *not* the demeanour of a man contemplating murder. His dress? As always impeccable; the murder weapon couldn't possibly have been in any of his pockets without causing attention. The time element? The length of time between Palmer leaving the table and the sounding of the alarm at the finding of the bullet-shattered broom cupboard door, could be measured in seconds; on the face of it Palmer hadn't had *time* to commit the murder.

The barrister for the Defence was a man wise in the subtle ways of a court of law. He knew the case for the Prosecution was weak, almost to the point of non-existence. He also knew that a surfeit of witnesses for the Defence was unnecessary, indeed probably counter-productive, it might irritate the judge and bore the jury. He could have called the Hodges. He could – despite Palmer's instructions – have called Peters. After the previous day's successful cross-examinations, he could have torn the Prosecution case to shreds by sheer weight of corroborative evidence. But in so doing he might have forfeited the sympathy of the court, and the man wasn't born who could foretell the verdict of a restless jury. The trick was to know when to stop. To know when the jury had heard enough, *and* enough for them to feel that the *Prosecution* had wasted their time in bringing the case in the first place.

The second day of the trial ended with the closing speeches

120

for the Prosecution and the Defence. Short speeches. Move and counter-move in the attempt to win over the court.

In the robing room after the court had been adjourned for the day the Defence barrister smiled and said, 'Care for a small side-bet?'

'No.' The Prosecution barrister returned the smile. 'The odds are too high.'

'A ridiculously weak case,' observed the Defence barrister.

'Indeed,' agreed the Prosecution barrister. 'But *somebody* shot him.'

'Quite, but from what I gather his death was no great loss to the human race.'

'There'll be others,' sighed the Prosecution barrister. 'However many die, there's never a vacuum.'

'Fortunately for us,' grinned the Defence barrister.

The judge's summing-up lasted almost two hours. He explained the law; he emphasised the principle of 'reasonable doubt'; he reminded the jury that their task was not to concern themselves with the question of who *had* murdered the dead man . . . that their only task was to decide whether or not Sidney Palmer had done the killing. He touched upon each witness, and the manner in which each witness had given evidence, what part of each witness's evidence might or might not have constituted a vital step towards a verdict of 'Guilty' or 'Not Guilty'. He ended by explaining to the jury that a 'majority verdict' was permissible, so long as the minority was not more than two; then added that he personally disliked 'majority verdicts' and that however long it might take them a 'unanimous verdict' was what he asked and hoped for.

The jury retired.

They were absent for more than two hours.

The Defence barrister looked a little worried; it was a rule-of-thumb whenever a jury retired on a criminal case that if a 'Not Guilty' verdict was to be reached, it was reached quickly; that the longer a jury was out the more likely it was that the verdict would be 'Guilty'.

The Prosecution barrister leaned across and whispered, 'I almost wish I'd taken that side-bet.'

He'd have lost.

Despite their prolonged absence the jury brought in a unanimous verdict of 'Not Guilty'. The judge thanked them. intimated that he shared their opinion, then smiled frostily at Sidney Palmer and pronounced him a free man.

Within minutes Sidney Palmer and his son, Eddie, were descending the broad shallow steps towards the pavement.

*

Sidney Palmer stood waiting while Eddie paid the driver of the taxi. He seemed unwilling to enter his own home; as if his prolonged absence in prison awaiting his trial had turned him into a stranger.

Eddie touched the elder man's arm, opened the door of the house, then led the way to the living room to where Freda was sitting in an armchair waiting.

Freda stared at her husband for a moment then said, 'Sidney,' in a low and colourless voice.

'Hello, pet.' Sidney Palmer's reply was equally soft-spoken and without emotion.

'What passion!' grinned Eddie. 'What an outburst of joy!'

Sidney and Freda Palmer ignored their son's teasing. More than that, they seemed almost unaware of his presence. Their eyes never left each other; a strangely sad gaze into which was crammed a small lifetime of suffering and disappointment.

Freda said, 'It's true, then?'

'Yes. I wouldn't be here otherwise.'

'No . . . of course not.'

'It's – it's been a long time.'

'Not as long as . . .' She paused, then murmured. 'I never thought you'd get away with it.'

'I was lucky.'

'Perhaps.'

'Very lucky.'

'I'm – I'm sorry.' For a moment she seemed to be on the point of breaking down. Then she swallowed and said, 'Truly . . . I'm sorry.'

'It's over.'

'I wonder.'

'Past.'

Sidney Palmer walked to the second armchair, lowered himself into it, rested his head against its back and closed his eyes. He seemed tired. Tired, almost to death.

Eddie said, 'Hey. What the hell?'

'It doesn't matter.' Sidney Palmer kept his eyes closed as he spoke.

123

'The hell it doesn't matter. What goes on?'

'No. Leave it. It's all . . .'

'It matters, pop. I'm the man who's asking. I'm your son for God's sake. I'm . . .'

Freda spoke to her husband. She said, 'It matters, love. He has to be told.'

'Told?' Eddie switched his gaze from one parent to the other. 'Told what?'

'Freda. It's not necessary. It's not . . .'

'Told *what*?' repeated Eddie.

'Sit down, Eddie.' Freda glanced at the sofa.

Eddie dutifully sat down on the sofa, then for the third time asked, 'Told what?'

'It was your gun, Eddie.' Sidney Palmer kept his eyes closed. His voice was little more than a whispered groan.

'Yeah. I know that. I recognised . . .'

'Didn't you ever wonder *why*?'

'Sure. But – y'know – I figured . . .'

'That you were the son of a murderer.'

'Hey, pop. I didn't say that. I didn't . . .'

'You are,' sighed Sidney Palmer. 'God help us, that's exactly what you are.'

'It was meant to be Peters.' The woman spoke the words. Faint words. Colourless words. Words which matched her eyes and her expression.

'What your mother did . . .' Sidney Palmer tilted his head, opened his eyes and stared at his son. 'What your mother did. Don't blame her. It was for your sake. For Daphne's sake.'

Freda repeated, 'It was meant to be Peters.'

'Will somebody tell me what the hell . . .'

'I was the one who shot him,' said Freda simply.

'Ma . . .' Eddie's jaw hung slack. 'Don't talk so . . . You're *crazy*. You? You're joking. How the hell . . .'

'No,' said Sidney gently. 'She's not joking. She thought it was Peters in the broom cupboard.'

'Oh, my God!'

Freda said, 'You were on stage, see? Everybody could see you. It *couldn't* be you. That's why.'

124

'Look . . .' Eddie seemed to make a great effort; seemed to force himself into the reality of the present and away from some personal Never-Never Land of comfortable self-delusion. He said, 'Okay. Let's have it. I don't know how. I don't know why. But I *want* to know.'

Freda glanced at her husband. Sidney Palmer moved his head in a tiny nod of acquiescence.

Freda took a deep breath then said, 'Valda – Mrs Hodge – let me in through the fire door at the end of the passage. About ten o'clock. I hid in the Ladies' toilets opposite the Gents'. I – I had the gun. Your gun. Valda – Mrs Hodge – arranged with the man called Rhodes that Peters would be in the broom cupboard. Locked in the cupboard. I couldn't have . . . Actually *looking* at him.'

'Peters,' said Eddie flatly.

'I thought it *was* Peters. We both . . . Valda – Mrs Hodge – thought it was Peters. It should have been Peters. That – that was what we arranged. Your signature tune, see? You were there on the stage, Eddie. It *couldn't* be you.' She paused, then continued, 'I went back into the Ladies' toilets. After I'd done it. She was going to let me out again. Through the fire door.'

'Valda?'

'Yes.'

'Bully for Valda.'

'It wasn't her fault, Eddie. It really wasn't. She – she got me away when the – er – the alarm was raised. She got me out.'

'But it *should* have been Peters?'

Freda nodded.

'And you.' Eddie turned to his father. 'Where do *you* fit into this crazy scheme?'

'As always, son.' Sidney Palmer tried to smile. 'I did the wrong thing. Something I shouldn't have done.'

'Such as going for a pee at the wrong moment?'

'And picking up the gun.' Once more the attempt to smile. The door of the Ladies' was open a few inches. I saw your mother and Mrs Hodge. Strange. I *knew*. Knew what had happened. Didn't know who'd been shot. But I recognised the gun and I saw your mother, so I knew. Guessed.'

'Uhuh.'

'Silence,' explained Sidney Palmer gently. 'That's all I could do, Eddie. That's all I *could* do. Not tell them about the gun. Not tell them about your mother. Not tell them *anything*, in case I said something likely to lead them in the right direction.'

' "Them", being the police?'

'Of course.'

'And "they",' said Eddie heavily, 'are going to nail you. Sooner or later . . . your card's already well and truly marked.'

'I don't see why you should think that. They're . . .'

'They're the Law, pop. They're right . . . even when they're wrong. They have you nailed. You're a murderer, you just happen to have beaten the system. That's not allowed, pop.'

'No! You're wrong. They make mistakes. They . . .'

'Okay. They've been *made* to make a mistake. They're not dumb. They can count beans. They'll *still* gun for you . . . if only because you've made 'em monkeys.'

'It's a risk,' admitted Sidney Palmer sadly. 'A necessary risk.'

'So?' Eddie's tone was contemptuous. 'Tell me something. Who's "got away with it"? Who? Not you. And Peters is still around.'

Softly, and without accusation, Sidney Palmer said, 'Don't forget something, Eddie. You provided the gun.'

Freda Palmer spoke after a prolonged silence.

She was near to tears as she said, 'I'm – I'm sorry, Eddie. I didn't mean . . .'

'Look, don't apologise to *me*!' It was an explosion. Part fear, part anger, part frustration. His voice was harsh with emotion. 'Apologise to him. He's the man who's been on trial. Who's been held in prison for doing damn-all. He's the poor sod who could have got life. My God! Talk about a cock-up. One kills. the other stands trial. And for what? For no good reason at all. Peters? He'll be laughing. Big joke. That louse still . . .'

126

'Eddie. Eddie.' Sidney Palmer tried to quieten the outburst. 'It's over. It's done with. You might have tried and you wouldn't have got away with it. Too many people knew. Too many people were waiting for it to happen. *You* wouldn't have been acquitted.'

And in the flat above *The Venus Fly-Trap* Tommy Hodge and Rhodes waited impatiently for the return of Valda Hodge. To say that Rhodes was on edge would be a gross exaggeration; such men have far too much self-control ever to be more than mildly irritated. But if Rhodes was moderately calm, Hodge took up any slack. For the past hour he'd chain-smoked and sipped his way through three healthy splashes of neat whisky.

Valda entered the flat and Hodge leaned forward in his chair expectantly. She walked through the lounge and towards the bedroom, peeling off her gloves and unfastening her coat. Both men watched her; Hodge with ill-concealed annoyance, Rhodes with a faint sardonic smile playing on his lips.

She returned to the lounge, flopped into an armchair, kicked off her shoes, stretched out a hand to take a cigarette from the box on a nearby side-table, lighted the cigarette, then blew a scarf of smoke towards the ceiling.

'And?' grunted Hodge.

' "Not Guilty",' she said brusquely.

'Jesus wept!'

'He played his cards well.' She wriggled her stockinged toes. 'We paid for a good lawyer, that's what we got.' She drew on the cigarette, then added, 'I could do with a drink.'

'Sure.' Rhodes moved towards a cabinet in one corner of the lounge. 'Whisky?'

'Gin with a fair measure of lime.'

Rhodes began to mix the drink.

Hodge said, 'We expected you sooner.'

'I walked around a little.'

'Eh?'

'Most of the way. Through the West End. I needed it.'

'You needed . . .'

'Fresh air,' she sighed. 'Enough time to convince myself that I hadn't helped to crucify a very nice guy.'

Hodge said, 'He got away with it.'

'The hell he did.' Rhodes carried the drink towards Valda. As he handed it to her, he added, 'That's the one thing that's out.'

'What's the difference?' Valda took the drink, tasted it, then said, 'The man you wanted stiffened . . . he's stiffened. That's the big thing.'

'Oh no, lady.'

'I don't see it.' Hodge frowned worried non-understanding. 'The way we played it . . .'

'Freda thought it was Peters,' said Valda wearily. 'She was conned. Okay – that gripes me a little, but I'll learn to live with it.'

'There's a difference,' murmured Rhodes.

Hodge said, 'I don't see it.'

'The way we played it. Not the way it came out.'

'The deal.' said Valda. 'That's what we're talking about.'

'Okay.' Rhodes nodded. 'The deal. It was meant to be one of those detective story things. The big, unsolved crime.'

'Look, if Palmer hadn't wanted to empty his bladder at that . . .'

'Ah, but he *did*,' smiled Rhodes.

Hodge said, 'So where's the difference?'

'Palmer.' Rhodes's voice was low and cold. 'The boys on the street. *They* matter. Not you, Hodge. Not the mugs who tool around with judges and juries. The unsolved crime, but not to the boys on the street. They always "know". No arrest – no trial . . . that means *I* did it. That's what was *meant* to happen. But now? Palmer. Sidney Palmer. The guy who can cool a big shot and beat the system.'

'For God's sake.' Valda's voice was heavy with disgust. 'He didn't cool anybody.'

'Yeah, *we* know that.' Rhodes's lips curled. 'But on the street? Lady, he did it. Court verdicts don't mean a damn thing to the people we're talking about. Palmer pulled it and walked away from it. That gives him size.'

Hodge blew out his cheeks, then said, 'For the record – for *my* record – why the hell didn't you feed her Peters? Why the big man? She wanted Peters . . .'

'She thought it was Peters,' interrupted Valda.

'If that damn door hadn't been closed and locked . . .'

'She'd *still* have thought it was Peters. She didn't know Peters from a hole in the head. and she was there to kill him, not to introduce herself.'

'So why the door? Why lock the guy in the . . .'

'Hey, Tommy.' Valda tasted her drink. Drew cigarette smoke into her lungs. Sounded weary of the whole affair. She said, 'Freda's a nice lady . . . remember? To look somebody in the face and pull a trigger? No way. She was shooting at a door. *That's* what she was doing. For Eddie. Maybe she could have pointed the gun at Peters. *Knowing* it was Peters. Maybe. Maybe not. It was too much of a gamble. So all she was asked to do was shoot a few holes in a door.'

'Peters,' mused Rhodes, 'is my problem.'

Valda looked a question.

Rhodes said, 'He's dumb, but little things have gone wrong. He's dumb, but not *that* dumb. He's starting to put building bricks together.'

'But the deal still stands?' Hodge was scared and it showed in his voice.

'Little man,' mocked Rhodes, 'I wouldn't have this joint free with cornflakes. Night clubs. Gambling joints. They're not my bag.'

'Except for a little thing called "Protection".' Valda matched his mockery tone for tone.

'That's a nasty word. Let's call it "Insurance".'

'Let's call it "Protection" and stop kidding each other.'

'Okay.' Rhodes grinned. 'You use your language. I'll use mine.'

'And now *you're* the big man.'

'You'd better believe that, lady.'

'Ah, well, silver linings aren't easy to come by.'

Hodge said, 'But you *are* the big man?'

'Yeah.' Rhodes's voice was a growling whisper. The grin had been replaced by hard-eyed determination. 'Things have screwed up a little. Not too much, but enough. The word on the street, already on the street at a guess, is that some creep of a head waiter can knock the big man and walk away. That's not good. That sounds a very sour note. And that note has to be sweetened.'

And in the Palmer home?

Tea and buttered scones. A few thought-filled silences. The calming influence of cigarette smoke. The rock-like foundation of a family that *was* a family. All these things helped. The anger had spent itself. The disgust had softened into dismay. Only the talk remained: the talk and the barely-understood fear.

Freda shook her head slowly and muttered, 'It should have been Peters. It was *meant* to be Peters.' She looked at her husband and said, 'Who was he anyway? I mean . . .'

'Don't mourn him, pet.' Sidney Palmer was wise enough to know the depth of her bewilderment. Softly, gently, he said, 'Him and his kind. It's what they deserve.'

'So easy eh?' murmured Eddie.

'No,' sighed Sidney. 'Not easy. Very difficult. More than that – very dangerous.'

'Pop, you don't know how . . .'

'Oh, yes, I *do*.' The tone silenced the younger man. 'I've worked alongside these people. Not on a stage. *There*. Within touching distance. Within hearing distance. And since before you were born. I've kept clean. I've bowed and scraped. I've steered clear of trouble. But don't tell me I don't *know*. I know, son, better than you do.'

'This family.' Freda wasn't too far from tears. 'A few months ago we were happy. Daphne, Eddie, you, me. A family, that's all. And now? What have we done? I mean, what have we *really* done?'

'We've stepped over a line, ma.'

'What? I don't understand. What sort of a . . .'

'He's right, pet. That's what we've done. Stepped over a line. I should have pleaded "Guilty".'

'But – but, Sidney, you *didn't*. I mean . . .'

'Did. Didn't.' Sidney Palmer looked sad. 'That's not important. That's not what matters.'

Eddie said, 'Ma, the mobs decide. It doesn't matter what the law says. They don't give a damn about the law. They don't come within the law. That's the line we mean. The law's on one side. They're on the other and we've crossed the line.'

'And – and can't get back?' breathed Freda.

'When they say, ma. Not before.'

'*If* they say,' added Palmer gently. 'And, if they need blood money, when that blood money's been paid.'

'If we told the police . . .'

'What? That *you* did the killing?'

Eddie said, 'Anyway, it wouldn't help. They'd just be more careful.'

'There must be something . . .'

'Ma,' pleaded Eddie, 'try to understand. Try. It should have been undetected. That's my guess. That or it should have been Peters. Peters wouldn't have mattered. But y'see, you shot a big wheel to death. The wrong man died for it not to matter.'

'If you hadn't brought that stupid gun home . . .'

'I know. And if Peters hadn't bought Daphne the car. And if Daphne hadn't killed herself. If – if – if. All those damned "ifs". If only you'd understood.'

'Eddie.' The tears glinted in her eyes. 'I did it for you.'

'Yeah, I know . . . I know . . .' Eddie Palmer closed his mouth, as if unwilling to give voice to his true feelings. He stood up and without another word walked from the room closing the door behind him.

Freda watched him.

Then she turned to her husband and stammered, 'Sidney, I . . .'

'It's all right. It's over,' comforted Sidney. 'It's gone and done with.'

'Is it?' she breathed.

*

131

It needed fifteen minutes to seven-thirty for the first opening of the doors and the trickle of early customers into the dining-cum-concert-room of *The Venus Fly-Trap*. The tables were ready; the cutlery, the crockery, the table-linen and the glassware spotless and waiting; the waiters were huddled in a corner, chatting in lowered voices and enjoying the last cigarettes before their business of weaving through the tables began. Behind the drawn curtain of the stage Eddie and *The Opus* were tuning and warming their instruments; at the bar the bar-keeps were polishing glasses already polished and occasionally watching their employer as he stood at the bar counter, sulky, silent and pouring booze down his throat at a steady speed which promised one hell of a consumption if he kept up the same rate of knots all evening.

Valda Hodge joined her husband at the bar. Concern and mild contempt jostled for position in her expression.

She said, 'Well?'

Hodge poured the last of the whisky down his throat and pushed the empty glass across the counter towards the nearest bar-keep. The bar-keep remained stone-faced, measured out a triple whisky, then added equal parts of iced water.

'Well?' repeated Valda.

Hodge tasted his new drink and remained silent.

'Are you trying to prove something?'

Hodge growled, 'Don't start what you can't finish, honey.'

'What's that supposed to mean?'

'You don't know?'

'Tommy.' Her voice was low-pitched. Soft enough not to reach the ears of the bar-keep, who'd moved a few yards along the counter. 'Getting smashed isn't the answer.'

'Forget it.' Once more the glass travelled to his lips.

'We paid for a good solicitor. A good barrister. What more could we do?'

'We're beautiful people,' sneered Hodge.

'No, not beautiful. Just people. And I got the hounds off your back, didn't I?'

'You did indeed.' The words were dull and without real meaning.

'This place.'

'Yeah . . . a nice place.'

'It's back where it belongs. With us.'

'Yeah, that too.'

'So where's the gripe?' she asked.

'The price might be a little high.'

'Come again?'

'Forget it, honey.' His voice was heavy with self-disgust; a self-disgust which was accentuated by the intake of booze.

'What the hell . . .'

'Live with your dreams, sweetheart. I'll ride the nightmares.'

'Palmer?' she asked, gently.

'Do *I* know somebody called Palmer?' he asked sarcastically.

'Sidney?'

'Sidney Palmer. Yeah, I've heard the name somewhere.'

'What happens?'

'Do I care?'

'Look, what the . . .'

'Am I *supposed* to know? Am I *supposed* to care?'

'Does he get his job back?'

'Since you ask . . . not in a million years.' Again the glass travelled to his lips.

'Why?'

'Because I hire and I fire.'

'I don't follow.'

'Honey . . . so many things.'

'He was found "Not Guilty". He *wasn't* guilty. It's not as if . . .'

'How right you are. It's not "as if".'

'Tommy, tell me.' Her voice was sombre. Worried. 'Am I missing something?'

'Yeah, your marbles.'

'That's no answer. That's no . . .'

'You and Palmer's wife. Both.'

'Hey, lover boy . . .'

Hodge growled, 'Let us say – if you need a reason – let

133

us say that Palmer has been in a holding prison for some few weeks. Eh? That his name has been mentioned in a few newspapers. Eh? That the gentlemen in blue uniforms have some small axe to grind. Eh? Let us say – if you need another reason – that the whiter-than-white clowns who frequent this dump might not like an ex-con serving up their wine and victuals. Let us say *that* . . . and leave everything else unsaid.'

'The hell. That's not fair . . .'

'We live in a very unfair world, honey. Didn't you know that?'

'Dammit, you know what I mean.'

'Yeah. I know what you mean . . . exactly.' More whisky-and-water found its way down his throat. 'But . . . y'know what? I am not too interested in what is fair. I am not too interested in what is foul. I am not too interested in any of these things. What *does* interest me? Just one small thing, sweetheart. I am interested in self-preservation. Nothing else.'

She stared at him, frowning.

She said, 'Tommy, you're choking on something.'

'No.'

'Don't con me, boy. I know your moods. I know . . .'

'Not choking. I have already choked.' His voice was soft and rasping as he continued, 'Now – as a personal favour – leave it. No more questions. Don't ask. There are things . . . reasons for reasons, and even reasons for *those* reasons. So, y'know, don't ask. Don't even touch. Just be glad. Be satisfied. You have damn near blown this place into outer space and a good man with it. Okay? And for that reason I wish to be left strictly alone in order that I might slowly and systematically get as pissed as a newt. That's what I want. That's *all* I want. With your permission – without your permission – that is my next move.'

She gazed at him for a moment, saw something in his eyes she didn't understand – something which frightened her a little – then she murmured, 'Okay, sweetheart. Just – when you surface, I'll be around.'

She walked away and left him to his sorrow.

Behind the curtains Eddie Palmer and *The Opus* were ready
for the opening bars of *Opus One*. Valda Hodge walked on to
the stage and said, 'Do you have a minute, Eddie?'

Eddie glanced at his watch.

Valda said, 'Be late for once in your life. It won't be the
end of the world.'

Eddie shrugged, motioned to the others to relax, then followed Valda into the wings; the narrow corridor which led
to the dressing rooms.

Valda said, 'I heard the verdict.'

'Yeah.' The reaction was cold and uncommittal.

'I'm glad.'

'That makes everything roses.'

'Eddie!'

'I'm glad, too.' There was controlled passion as he pushed
the words past an almost rigid jaw. 'I'm glad about some
things. Other things . . . they make me puke.'

'You – er – you know,' she said cautiously.

'Yeah. I know.'

'How's your mother taking it?'

'Great. She's knitting daisy chains.'

'Eddie, I'm serious.'

'Me? I'm busting a gut laughing.'

'Please, Eddie. How's she taking it?'

'Badly. How else?'

'And Sidney?'

'Oh, for Christ's sake!'

'Get off it, Eddie. I'm asking.'

'He'll need work,' growled Eddie.

'I know.' She frowned her embarrassment.

'He's a good head waiter.'

'I know that, too.'

'It's the only job he knows.'

'Don't ask,' she murmured softly. Sadly.

'Tommy?'

'No. Don't try Tommy.'

'Why?'

'*The Fly-Trap* can't use him, Eddie.'

'It follows.' Eddie's mouth curled.

'Eddie . . . don't blame him. Please.'

'Who? Who don't I blame?'

'Tommy. He – he . . .' She floundered and ran out of words.

'I don't blame Tommy.' He paused, then it came out in a flood. 'Dammit, I don't blame *anybody*. Ma, you, pop . . . everybody screwing things up, trying to help. Nobody to blame. But that doesn't ease things.'

'Freda,' said Valda. 'Is she at home in the afternoon?'

'Yeah.'

'Every afternoon?'

'Yeah, she rarely goes out.'

'Would you mind if I called?' The question was gentle. Anxious.

'No more fancy ideas, eh?'

'No more fancy ideas,' she promised.

'I mean it. I don't want her to . . .'

'Another shoulder for her tears,' interrupted Valda. 'That's all. It might help.'

'Yeah.' Eddie glanced at his watch. 'Who knows? It might help. Now, if you'll excuse me, I have music to make.'

Tuesday, November 7th

Half a dozen spins of Mother Earth. In Oxford Street the stores were flexing their muscles for the annual Christmas spending bonanza. In open spaces the two-day-old litter of bonfires had still to be cleared. At the Cenotaph and at the Royal Albert Hall preparations were in progress for a nation's remembrance of the dead of two world wars and, in thousands of homes throughout the land, ex-servicemen were hunting in drawers for medals to be worn on some parade of sadness.

Like the ticking of a clock – like the passing of the seasons – the yearly rigmarole went its way.

In *The Venus Fly-Trap* the adverts for that extra oomph demanded by Yuletide and the New Year were already displayed. Money was going to flow and Soho and the clubs of Soho saw no good reason why a few gallons of that money shouldn't flow in the right direction. The booze was stocked high in the cellars. The turkeys were packed tight in the deep freezers. The puddings were given extra shelf-room in the stores.

The strippers, the torch singers, the blue comedians, the various 'groups' . . . Jesus, if you didn't work from mid-December until mid-January, you really *were* on the down slope. The once-a-year-big-cherry was ripening and almost ready for taste.

Tommy and Valda Hodge were easing their way through the evening observance of sprucing up ready for opening time. Tommy carried a glass around with him as he moved from bedroom to bathroom, from bathroom back to bedroom, from bedroom to lounge. Their conversation and style of conversation told its own story; strictly speaking not unfriendly – strictly speaking not contemptuous – strictly

137

speaking nothing too much out of the ordinary, but strictly speaking very different from what it had once been.

'You ordered the trees?' asked Valda.

'Trees?' Tommy adjusted the waistband of his trousers slightly, he was growing the hint of a paunch.

'Trees. Christmas trees.'

'Oh, yeah. Sure.'

'Two?'

'Two. We decided on two. I ordered two.'

'And the trimmings? The baubles?'

'Look, I said I ordered. I ordered.'

'Fine.' Valda wielded a comb and did things to her hair. 'Only last year . . .'

'The hell with last year. This year we're organised.'

'Sure.'

Tommy looked at his wife's face reflected in the dressing-table mirror.

He said, 'You think I'm dumb?'

'Did I say that?'

'I think you think I'm dumb,' said Tommy gruffly.

'I think you're taking in too much juice. That's what *I* think.'

'A little drink now and . . .'

'No. Not now and again, Tommy. All the time. A little drink that lasts forever.'

'I can hold it.'

'Yeah, the motto of every lush who ever lived.'

Tommy growled, 'I'm no lush.'

'You damn soon will be.' She paused, lowered the comb, turned from the dressing-table and in a low voice said, 'Tommy, you can't drown it. You either live with it or forget it. That . . . or take him back.'

'I dunno what . . .'

'Knackers!' She spat the word at him. Her patience seemed suddenly to run out. 'Tommy Hodge, I'm Valda. I'm the woman who knows you. Better than you know yourself. You know damn well what I'm talking about. Sidney Palmer, the guy who could have slapped *me* behind bars.'

138

'And his own missus.'

'That, too,' she agreed. 'But what I did was for you. To get the hounds away from your arse.'

'What *she* did was for her son. What *he* did was for his wife. So who owes who favours?'

'You're trying,' she sneered. 'That much . . . you're trying.'

'What?'

'To convince yourself. That *you* don't owe a thing to anybody.'

He tasted the whisky.

'More courage?' she jeered.

'Why the hell should I be scared?'

'Okay, why *are* you scared?'

'Four people. Eh? You. Palmer and his wife. Rhodes. I could drop you . . . any of you, all of you. Ever think of that? Murder. And if not murder some side-issue to murder. Why the hell should *I* be scared?'

'Well . . . not of me,' she murmured.

'You bet your sweet life, honey.'

'Not of the Palmers.'

'Screw the Palmers.'

'So that leaves . . . who?' Her smile was taunting. Contemptuous.

'Forget it,' he muttered.

She placed the comb on the surface of the dressing-table. It was a deliberate – almost controlled – action. She stood up, walked to him, then stopped and kissed him full on the lips. It wasn't a lover's kiss. Nor was it a wife's kiss. Rather it was the kiss of a mother comforting her frightened child.

All anger and contempt had left her as she said, 'What worries you, worries me, honey. Okay. we scratch at each other's eyeballs, occasionally. That's us. The way we're made You don't need booze any more than I do. Together . . . that's all. We can take the world. Rhodes? An animal? Okay, an animal. It makes no difference, honey. Animals – any animal – can be tamed. If not tamed, destroyed.'

'You think so?' There was utter disbelief in the question. That, plus bitterness and self-pity.

139

'Ask Rhodes,' she said softly. 'I put him where he is. I can just as easily push him off the pedestal.'

A few minutes to midnight. A few minutes to another day. The night people had taken over occupancy of Piccadilly Circus. The night people: pale-faced and hollow-eyed; gaunt and haunted as they trudged their way through their own peculiar nightmares, seeking some twisted Arcadia they themselves could never describe.

Above ground and under ground. They swarmed and jostled along the pavements, spilling into the road. They sought darkened corners and doorways in which to inject into their arms that which was killing them, but that which they needed in order to live. The zombies of the civilised world . . . the only true zombies. The only true 'walking dead'.

There was little traffic about. Those who knew re-routed their journeys rather than drive through this haunt of after-dark Bedlamites. Even the London cabbies: few of them would willingly drive through this unholy mob and none of them would either pick up or put down passengers within sight of Piccadilly Circus.

The 'Dilly' of old was a place only remembered.

Sidney Palmer was there in the thick of it before he was even aware of the fact. He'd walked; walked aimlessly since dusk. Part of his mind remembered the Victoria Embankment; the river on his left reflecting the lights from the opposite bank; the right turn up Northumberland Avenue, Trafalgar Square, then Haymarket. And now Piccadilly Circus at close on midnight.

Despite the bustle and the manner of men and women who made up the aimlessly milling groups, winding along pavements and carriageway alike, Sidney Palmer saw no reason to be afraid. Piccadilly – Soho – one was no worse than the other. The difference – if there was a difference – was that between amateur and professional. In Soho fortunes were made via the provision of vice and perversion. In Piccadilly vice and perversion equated with 'kicks'. In Soho it

140

was organised and hidden. In Piccadilly it was noisy and spontaneous.

Nevertheless, Freda would be worrying.

He turned right along Coventry Street, keeping his eyes open for a cruising cab. At the same time he glanced through the glass frontage of the late-night cafés and snack-bars. Saw the garish and sometimes not too clean interiors wherein the night people sought warmth for the price of something which gave them the right to sit at a table. The sight saddened him. So much youth burning its way into premature age. Such a loss. Such a waste. So much basic and pointless madness.

Then he stopped. Stared through the glass at the dimly lit interior. His heart seemed to rise and threaten to choke him. He couldn't believe . . . and yet to disbelieve would be to deny the sight of his own eyes.

All right . . . she had her back to him. Only occasionally as she turned to speak to one of her companions did he see a part-profile. But the belted mac. The hair style. It had to be her. It *was* her!

Therefore what had Eddie seen? Eddie had been mistaken . . . terribly, terribly mistaken. It was possible. Eddie had never seen a corpse before. And, dammit, they only had Eddie's word. All Freda and he had seen was a coffin. Therefore . . .

He pushed open the swing-door. Walked almost on tiptoe, towards the table. He stopped behind her back but within easy speaking distance.

He breathed, 'Daphne.'

The girl turned, and it wasn't Daphne. And he felt a fool. Once he could actually *see* her it was obvious. She didn't look like Daphne at all.

The girl stared at him and said, 'You talking to me?'

'I'm – I'm sorry.'

The girl was chewing gum. Her jaws worked rhythmically. Her eyes were hard and worldly-wise.

She said, 'What was it you wanted, old man?'

'N-nothing. I . . .'

One of her companions – the youth in the soiled safari-jacket – scowled, and said, 'Jerk off, creep. She ain't a pick-up.'

'I – I never thought for a moment . . .'

'I'll bet.' The lips, as they moved with the chewing jaw, curled into a sneer.

'I assure you, miss . . .'

The youth snarled, 'Piss off.'

'Yes.' Sidney Palmer bobbed his head. 'It's – it's just that . . .'

'That you picked the wrong chick.' The youth ended the sentence.

'No, not that.'

The youth placed his half-smoked cigarette carefully in the scooped-out indentation on the rim of the cheap ashtray.

Palmer stammered, 'I – I thought you were . . . a friend. Somebody I knew. From outside – from the pavement . . .'

The youth said, 'Pick a bag from some other party, goat-balls. Try one nearer your own age.'

He pushed himself upright menacingly.

Palmer whispered, 'I'm sorry.'

He turned and walked from the café. Without looking round he knew the girl and the youth were watching. Ready – eager – for trouble.

Thursday, November 9th

It was a grey afternoon; the shade of grey usually associated by provincials with London itself. A gunmetal sky. Roads and pavements still wet from a recent shower. The cold of oncoming winter already touched the capital; in the offices of the city the radiators pushed small warmth towards the office workers and in the living room of a house in Poplar two women sat huddled before an electric fire and stumblingly tried to smooth out an awkward, stunted conversation.

Valda said, 'I suppose you should hate me. I wouldn't blame you.'

'What good?' murmured Freda.

'You thought it was Peters.'

'It wouldn't matter.'

'I'm sorry?'

'Today . . . it wouldn't matter.'

'Oh!'

'For Eddie's sake,' explained Freda. 'That's all. To stop *him*.'

'Er – yes.' Valda nodded.

'It's just Sidney,' sighed Freda.

'I'm sorry about that, too.'

'It's not your fault.'

'I've tried,' said Valda gently.

'What?'

'Tommy won't wear it. He won't give him his job back.'

'No . . . not that.'

'What, then?'

'It's Eddie and Sidney. They seem to know these things.'

'What things?'

Freda hesitated, then said, 'The gangsters.'

'Y'mean Rhodes?'

'I suppose.'

'What about Rhodes?'

'Eddie and Sidney. They seem to expect something.'

'No.' Valda shook her head. 'I'd know.'

'Perhaps,' sighed Freda.

'Is he out?' asked Valda.

'Who?'

'Sidney.'

'Walking. Walking the streets . . . showing them.'

'Who?'

'The men. The men he should be afraid of.'

'Oh!'

'Looking for work. Showing them he *isn't* afraid.'

'Okay then.' Valda tried to smile. 'He's okay.'

But her words had some room for worried uncertainty.

The truth of it was that even Sidney Palmer hadn't appreciated the full extent of their influence. Soho . . . okay, he hadn't really *expected* work within Soho. He'd tried – after all he was known as a top-class head waiter within the area surrounding *The Venus Fly-Trap* – but even as he'd asked, he'd known the answer.

'Sorry, Palmer. No vacancies.'

'Just as an ordinary waiter, perhaps?'

'You know how it is, Palmer.'

'Good waiters aren't easy to come by.'

'I can keep staff.'

'Some. But the younger ones come and go. I know how it is.'

'No vacancies, Palmer.'

'Look, all I'm asking . . .'

'Palmer be told. Don't make me draw diagrams.'

'So? *That's* how it is?'

'No vacancies, Palmer. Don't come back.'

That. and variations upon the same exchange, had filled his first couple of days looking for employment. It hadn't been a surprise. Indeed, it would have been a surprise had it been otherwise. Sidney Palmer knew his Soho; knew the slim line which separated the 'non-syndicate' clubs and restaurants from those controlled, directly or indirectly, by the mobs. Owners, proprietors, managers, front men . . . the word had gone out. 'Nobody employs Palmer.' It had been enough. It had been a waste of breath and a waste of shoe leather.

Sidney Palmer had sighed, accepted the inevitable and moved farther afield.

Valda said, 'Not a nice thing, this.'

'What?' Freda didn't understand.

'Waiting.'

'Waiting. Y'know . . . just waiting.'

'For Sidney?'

'It can't be nice for you.'

'He needs work.'

'Sure. But . . .' Valda relapsed into awkward silence.

'He'll find it, somewhere.'

'Oh, sure.'

In a gentle, wistful voice Freda said, 'I think he sees it as a gesture.'

'Work?'

'No. Being out like this. Visiting places. To show them he isn't frightened.'

'A nice guy,' said Valda quietly.

'I think so.'

Having exhausted Soho Sidney Palmer had moved into the Tottenham Court Road–Oxford Street district. It had been hard to tell. The best places . . . it seemed inconceivable that *they* were mob-dominated. And yet . . .

'I'm sorry. Not without references.'

'Mr Hodge. *The Venus Fly-Trap.* If you ring him, I'm sure he'd . . .'

'Written references, I'm afraid.'

'I – er – I don't think . . .'

'Necessary, I'm afraid, Mr Palmer.'

'You too?' The question had had a hint of bitterness.

'I beg your pardon?'

'You don't know what I'm talking about, of course.'

'No. I'm afraid I don't.'
'I wonder.'
'I'm sorry. I'm not . . .'
'Thanks for seeing me.'
'Not at all, Mr Palmer. If we could . . .'
'Ah, yes. If you *could*.'

Hodge was still drinking more than his usual intake. Perhaps not quite as much as he'd been slopping down his throat at the time when his wife had pulled him up short. But enough. Enough to put a slight slur on his speech. Enough to make his eyes a little out of focus. Enough.

He sipped neat whisky at the bar of *The Venus Fly-Trap*, watched the waiters putting the finishing touches to the tables prior to their pre-opening-time break, and saw Eddie Palmer stroll from the door leading to the dressing rooms.

He called, 'Hey, kid. C'mon and join me.'

Eddie turned his head, hesitated, then joined Hodge at the bar.

'Drink?' asked Hodge.

'Why not?'

'Sure. That's what I say, kid. Why the hell not?'

Hodge poured what was left of his own drink down his throat, splashed a good re-fill from a bottle at his elbow, then poured neat whisky into a second glass and pushed it towards Eddie.

Hodge raised his glass and muttered, 'Here's to all the nice guys.'

'I'll drink to that.' Eddie touched his lips with the whisky.

Hodge said, 'Y'know what? There's not many left.'

'Nice guys?'

'Collector's items. Wouldn't you say?'

'Moving that way,' agreed Eddie.

'Good people . . . eh?'

'They're around.'

'They need finding though, eh?'

'Maybe.'

Hodges mumbled, 'You and your old man.'

'I'm biased.' smiled Eddie.

'Good people.'

'If you say so.'

'Bloody collector's items.'

'You should put us up for auction.'

'Don't be like that, Eddie.' Hodge scowled.

'Now? What should I say?'

'Nice people.'

'Okay . . . nice people,' agreed Eddie.

'Not like me.' Hodge tasted whisky. 'Me? I am what I am.'

'Okay. What are you?'

'I am what I am. That's what. What I am.'

'So sure?'

'I know, kid. I *know*.'

'Congratulations.'

'A bastard,' muttered Hodge.

'Who?'

'Me. Most people. When it comes to their skin they're bastards.'

'Could be,' agreed Eddie gently.

'Yeah. But not Sidney.' Hodge squinted into Eddie's face. 'You know Sidney?'

'It's a safe bet.'

'Your old man.'

'Yeah.'

'A nice guy.'

'You don't need a show of hands.'

'Too nice.'

Eddie sipped his drink and didn't answer.

Hodge muttered, 'A little too nice . . . eh?'

'Sometimes.'

'But the rest of us . . . bastards.'

Freda said, 'Tea?'

'What?' Valda started. For all of three minutes neither woman had spoken; each deep in her own thoughts. Valda clicked her mind to the there and then. She said, 'No. No, thanks.'

'I could easily brew some.'

'No. Not for me, thanks.'

Freda shrugged.

Valda chose her words and said, 'You're beyond me, honey.'

'What? How?' Freda looked mildly surprised.

'You aren't worried. Aren't afraid. Nothing.'

'I killed a man,' said Freda tonelessly.

'It was what he deserved,' said Valda. Then she lied and said, 'We both thought it was Peters.'

'Who was he?'

'A name, that's all I know.' This time she told the truth.

'One of the gangster people?'

'Uhuh.' Valda nodded.

'But a human being.'

'In the widest sense.' Valda smiled sadly. 'Don't mourn him, honey. Think about your own man.'

'He'll be all right,' said Freda confidently.

'I wish I could be as sure.'

'Why not?'

'They make their own rules. Pretty well as they go along.'

'They?'

'The mobsters. The "gangster people" as you call them.'

'And Sidney?'

'Christ knows. I only wish he'd get back.'

'He'll be here soon.'

The hash-houses. The snack-bars. The two- and three-man all-night sandwich joints. There was bloody-minded desperation in Sidney Palmer's search for work within the catering trade. The hell with it, there had to be *something*. Something, *somewhere*. A capital city, with restaurants and cafés in damn near every street, there had to be *something*. The heavies couldn't control them all. Indian, French, Italian, Chinese, Turkish – every country under the sun had its own eating-house – there had to be *something*.

That a mild-mannered man like Sidney Palmer could be driven to such all-consuming determination was, perhaps, proof of . . . what? Of the steel buried deep inside every human being? Of a universal threshold of tolerance beyond which every man turned and fought his tormentors? Of some basic madness which refused to accept defeat?

Certain it is that Sidney Palmer while seeking employment was also doing something else. There was an extra 'something' other than the need to work which drove him forward.

Nevertheless it was a madness.

It was a madness which by this time had brought him to the ridiculous ploy of trudging the streets – turning and twisting without predetermined pattern – and calling in at all and every establishment where even the bare possibility of employment presented itself. And with each refusal the accompanying madness grew, the belief that the whole of the capital's catering industry was controlled by faceless men wielding unimaginable power.

He was in streets he'd never walked before. Streets leading from side-streets. Narrow streets. Little-known streets which formed a maze behind the façade of 'London' as the majority of people knew that city.

It was late afternoon. Bleak. Inhospitable. The light was waning and he walked a rubbish-strewn pavement. The street was deserted and this, perhaps is why he noticed the car as it nosed its way around a corner. A big car; wide wheel-based and needing most of the space between the two kerbs. There was a menace about the manner in which it was being driven; about its gradual increase in speed; about the way in which it seemed to come at him, like a killer stalking its prey and winding itself up to pouncing pace.

At first Palmer refused to believe the evidence of his eyes. Then, as the wheels of the car mounted the pavement less than fifteen yards away, Palmer saw the face of the driver. Peters. Leaning forward in his seat. Grinning. Leering. Easing the car within six inches of the nearside wall.

Palmer moved. He sprinted away from the approaching car and hurled himself into the safety of the rear doorway of

149

some unknown premises. The car seemed almost to touch the heel of his shoe, and as it passed Peters sounded the horn in a long, disappearing blast – like the idiot laughter of somebody, something certain of eventual success.

Palmer was trembling. He leaned against the brickwork of the doorway, clenched his fists by his side and inhaled deep breaths in an attempt to control himself.

Without a doubt it had been an attempted killing. The manner in which the car had been driven, the deserted back street and, finally, the expression on Peters's face left no doubt as to the serious cold-blooded attempt to run him down. To smear him against the wall. Which, in turn, meant that they *knew*. Somebody *knew*. The coincidence of the car, Peters and himself all being in this near-unknown street was something which could be dismissed without a second thought. Which in turn meant he'd been followed. Shadowed. Peters – whoever Peters worked for, God only knew how many 'watchers' – had been following his every move.

Why?

To eliminate him . . . why else?

He was a threat. He knew things dangerous men were unwilling to risk him knowing. The shooting at *The Venus Fly-Trap*. What else? Why else would they want to kill him?

Eventually he controlled his trembling. He peeped from his shelter into the empty street. He hurried – almost ran – to the nearest corner. Turned right. Then left. Then right again . . . and into a road carrying a moderate amount of traffic; on to pavements used by hurrying pedestrians.

Only then did he feel safe.

He flagged a passing taxi, climbed in and said, 'Soho. *The Venus Fly-Trap.*'

It took some telling. Freda listened and Sidney Palmer chose his words very carefully, in order not unduly to alarm his wife. And that, too, was an impossibility. To tell your wife that you've escaped being deliberately run down by a motor car and expect her not to worry too much. That presupposes

150

that there is no love and no imagination. No love, no imagination . . . no marriage in the real sense.

Therefore Freda was *very* worried.

'And Tommy Hodge?'

'That didn't do much good.' Palmer smiled bitterly.

'But surely he could . . .'

'He was too drunk to understand.'

'Oh!'

'Anyway.' Palmer pulled a face. 'What can *he* do?

'He's one of them.'

'Oh, no.' Palmer shook his head. 'I know him too well. He's . . .'

'His wife was here earlier.'

'Mrs Hodge?'

'Valda.'

'I didn't think . . .'

'Why she came, I don't know. There seemed to be no real . . .'

'She's kind-hearted.'

'What she said,' insisted Freda. 'Not in as many words. Hints . . . that's all.'

'What sort of hints?'

'Worried that you were out. As if she knew.'

'Pet, I doubt whether . . .'

'As if she knew something might have happened to you.'

Palmer ran his fingers through his hair.

Freda said, 'All right. We leave London.'

'What?' Palmer looked startled at the suggestion.

'There are other restaurants. Hotels. In the provinces, where these men can't reach you.'

'We leave London?' Palmer stared, as if still unable to believe the seriousness of the suggestion.

Freda said, 'It's not the world.'

'It's *our* world. Where we were born. Where we've always lived.'

'It's also their world,' said Freda mildly.

'And you're frightened? As frightened as that?'

'Weren't you?' she asked. 'When Peters tried to kill you with the car. Weren't you . . .'

'They – they won't do it again.'

'From what Valda says . . .'

'Damn Valda!' It was a minor explosion of irritation. Out of character, therefore a pointer to his undoubted worry. 'She wants her cake, she wants to eat it. You thought you were shooting Peters. She helped you. She *says* she thought you were shooting Peters. That may be true. It may *not* be true. That's unimportant. The fact is, you killed somebody much more important than Peters will ever be . . . and *that's* why I'm being intimidated.' He cooled down, then in a calmer tone continued, 'Hodge was drunk. But he wasn't *too* drunk. Y'know, pet,' a smile flirted with his lips. '*Not* being employed by a man has certain advantages. You can speak your mind. Peters still visits *The Fly-Trap*. Tommy Hodge will pass on the message. Anything else . . . any other attempt at running me down. The same with you. And Eddie. Anything! I go to the police.'

'Sidney. That means me. That means . . .'

'That means Valda,' said Palmer grimly. 'They'll question *her*. Your name won't be mentioned. Except by Valda, and they won't believe that. But other names will be mentioned.'

'Eddie's, for example,' said Freda.

'Probably,' agreed Palmer. 'That's a chance I'm prepared to take. It's – it's a matter of proof. I don't think they can prove anything against Eddie. He was on the stand at the time, he should be able to clear himself completely. But the others. Whoever they are. Rhodes . . . any of them. Peters . . . whoever they are. I think the police might be interested.' He stared at her and ended, 'They frighten us. Or we frighten them. It's one or the other. And if Tommy Hodge and his wife suffer . . . who cares? We don't owe them a thing. They started all this. He could have banned Daphne from *The Fly-Trap*. He wouldn't, and that's where it all started. I don't feel sympathy. I don't feel anything. But – whoever they are – they'd better get off our backs, otherwise the Law steps in.'

Friday, November 10th

But Hodge knew it was a waste of time.

He was sober. Deliberately sober. Somewhere along the line he – Valda – had taken too big a mouthful. Nor could he spit any of it out. It had to be swallowed, even if it choked him. The old adage, concerning long spoons and the devil, had never been more appropriate. He – Valda – was part of it; in there up to the eyeballs; involved in a gangland vendetta which could still see its climax in a charge of murder. Murder and the various appendices to murder.

All he'd wanted was a club. All his life: the one ambition from which he'd never deviated. A top club here in Soho, one of the 'name' clubs of the capital. That's all he'd wanted, that and nothing more.

And he'd made it.

Jesus Christ . . . less than six months ago. *The Venus Fly-Trap.* One of the class joints. A place with its own 'feel'. With its own atmosphere. With its own brand of service and entertainment. The small-combo jazz buffs had begun to know it; had begun to list Eddie Palmer and *The Opus* as one of the 'musts' whenever the loot in their pocket allowed them the luxury of a night on the town. But more than that, even. The gamblers, too. The people who wanted to spin the wheel or turn the cards . . . the gambling room of *The Venus Fly-Trap* always gave them a fair deal. Nothing was ever rigged. The 'house take' was moderate and, on a lucky streak, the winnings were ample enough to bring them back to the tables again and again. And the rest – the common-or-garden night-outers – they, too, were catered for. Good food. good wine and good table-service. The occasional stripper to make them feel 'cosmopolitan' and a little naughty, but strippers who knew their business and didn't put on a solo fornication routine; strippers with the required artistry to

153

make their act happy, a little provocative, but never lewd. And groups to provide an interlude of non-jazz variety; hand-picked groups who were never too far out in their dress or their contortions; groups who knew enough about music – groups who *played* music – groups who didn't chase the jazz fans out of the place. The same with the solo-spot singers. Sometimes out-and-out jazz, sometimes torch-type, some-times ballad warblers; but always within the spectrum of top class moderation. Even the comics. Okay, blue boys – but the customers expected blue-tinged gags – but always clever. No filth. No out-and-out dirt. Bawdy . . . okay, bawdy. But no lavatory-wall muck.

Christ, everything – *everything* – had been put through a personal sieve of acceptability. To get that peculiar – that very unique – *Venus Fly-Trap* touch. Nor had it been easy. It had meant looking for a very fine balance. Paying for the best and insisting upon the best. And more than that . . . accepting what *you* counted as best. Telling the agents and the P.R. outfits to go screw themselves. Taking nobody's word about *anything*.

And he'd made few mistakes. *His* taste had been the taste shared by enough people to guarantee success. To put money in the bank. To dream dreams of an early retirement in the sun, where the taxman didn't want ten pints of blood every damn year; where he could stroll through the rest of his life with Valda without penny-pinching, and not too old to enjoy the good things of life.

That . . . less than six months ago.

And since then?

Thanks to that pebble-brained little bitch, Daphne Palmer. Thanks to Peters and his ever-open zip. Thanks to Rhodes and his yen for power. Thanks to Valda and her refusal to let things simmer along at their own pace. Thanks to that damn fool Eddie, and his tooling around with a shooter. Thanks to Palmer's wife and her urge to pump bullets through broom-cupboard doors.

A whole basketful of goodies, and they were all *his*.

And now, to cap the cake, this 'and-or-else' garbage from

Sidney Palmer. A bloody messenger-boy between an out-of-work waiter and a would-be big-shot mobster.

Holy Cow! All he'd ever wanted was a sweet little club. All he'd ever worked for. All he'd ever schemed for.

And now this . . .

At Table Twenty-Seven Rhodes pushed himself upright. He dabbed his lips with the napkin, placed the napkin on a side-plate, then quietly crossed the room to where Tommy Hodge was waiting.

On stage Eddie Palmer and *The Opus* were swinging into a fast tempo version of *Sweet Georgia Brown*; a good, foot-tapping arrangement which had the customers smiling in appreciation.

Tommy Hodge was within the shadow of one of the alcoves used by himself and Valda to survey the dining-cum-concert-room without attracting attention.

Rhodes joined him and said, 'The waiter said you wanted to see me.'

'Uhuh.' Hodge nodded and stared past Rhodes's shoulder. 'Well?'

'A favour, Mr Rhodes,' said Hodge awkwardly.

Rhodes waited.

Hodge said, 'You're not going to like it, but . . .'

'In that case you won't get it,' said Rhodes calmly.

Hodge took a deep breath then said, 'At least let me ask.'

'Sure.' Rhodes nodded.

Hodge said, 'The head waiter. Palmer. Sidney Palmer.'

'He *was* the head waiter,' corrected Rhodes.

'Yeah.' Hodge swallowed then said, 'Peters has tried to kill him.'

Rhodes looked mildly interested.

'To run him down with a car,' said Hodge.

'So?'

'Was he . . .' Hodge rubbed his lips with his fingers. 'Was he acting on orders?'

'Orders from who?'

'I thought maybe . . . you.'

155

'Me?' Rhodes looked surprised.

'Well, y'know . . .' stammered Hodge, then closed his mouth.

'That's what you thought?' Rhodes slipped a cigarette case from an inside pocket. Selected a cigarette.

'It's – it's just that . . .'

As he returned the case to its pocket and flicked a lighter, Rhodes drawled, 'That's a very bad habit, Hodge.'

'Eh?'

'Thinking things like that.' Rhodes lighted the cigarette. 'Having those sort of thoughts. They're not healthy.'

'He – he should be told,' stumbled Hodge.

'The head waiter?'

'No. Peters. Peters should be told.'

'So why tell me?'

'What?'

'Something . . . Peters needs telling. Why tell me?'

'Mr Rhodes,' groaned Hodge. 'I'm trying to help. Believe me.'

'Sure . . . why not?' Rhodes blew smoke past Hodge's left ear.

Hodge breathed, 'He's – he's threatened to blow the whistle.'

For a moment Rhodes's eyes narrowed, then he murmured, 'In detail, Hodge.'

'It – it happened, yesterday. Peters trying to run down Palmer. Palmer came here. To see me. To pass a message.'

'To Peters?'

'To – to . . .' Hodge moved his shoulders. 'To whoever it might concern.'

'As the saying goes.'

'Yeah.' Hodge nodded. 'He opens his mouth about the shooting if it happens again.'

'That, I doubt,' smiled Rhodes.

'No. He swore . . .'

'He has a wife, Hodge.'

'Yeah, I know. But . . .'

'Middle-class morality.' Rhodes waved the cigarette and

grinned. 'G. B. Shaw knew his onions. Middle-class morality. You don't know human nature, Hodge.'

'And if you're wrong?' asked Hodge breathlessly.

'I'm not wrong.'

'*If* you're wrong,' insisted Hodge. 'He's not the only man with a wife.'

'You?' Rhodes raised sardonic eyebrows.

'She's in it. *You're* in it, Rhodes.'

'Y'know,' mused Rhodes, 'I could sue you for that.'

'Dammit, you . . .'

'Not a thing, friend.'

'For Christ's sake!'

'A man was shot. Here in your club. The fuzz thought your head waiter pulled the trigger. I hear things. I hear he was covering for his wife. I hear *your* wife arranged the set-up. I hear the wrong mug was corpsed. I hear things . . . that's all.'

'If you think Valda . . .'

'*You* kill him,' said Rhodes calmly.

'Eh?' Hodge's jaw dropped.

'You have a lot to lose . . . a wife for example. Okay, you kill him.'

'I – I don't want him killed.'

'What else?' Rhodes sounded gently surprised. Gently amused.

'Look, just a word with Peters.'

'Assuming Peters is working solo.'

'Oh!'

'Isn't he?' asked Rhodes softly.

'I dunno. How the hell do I know?'

'I'm sorry, Hodge.' Rhodes grinned.

'What?'

'I thought you had it all figured out.'

'Look, all I know is . . .'

'Sending for me. Not Peters.'

'Look . . .' Hodge took a deep breath, then said, 'Mr Rhodes. I don't want anybody killed. Not Palmer. Not Peters. Nobody. And I don't want Palmer's wife sent to prison,

157

because if she goes, my wife goes. All I'm asking. Get Peters away from Palmer. That's all *he's* asking. It's not a lot.'

'Yeah, but he's asking *me*.'

'No. *I'm* asking you. That's the favour.'

'It still assumes things.'

'Yeah, that you can do it.'

'A big assumption.'

'I don't think so.'

'No?'

'I didn't come with the morning's milk, Mr Rhodes.'

Rhodes smiled.

Hodge said, 'You can do it. One word, that's all it needs.'

'I'll think about it.' Rhodes drew on the cigarette. 'That's all, Hodge. Think about it . . . see if I can remember that word you have in mind.'

Sunday, November 12th

As almost always on Remembrance Sunday it was cold and wet. As always the world – and London in particular – seemed to slow its pace a little. As if for that one Sunday of the year the weight of the dead of two world wars required more carrying than usual. As if at least one generation *really* remembered. *Really* knew the meaning of international madness.

In the Palmer home Freda, Sidney and Eddie had watched the wreaths being placed around the Cenotaph, had watched the monarch lead the nation in its homage to those who had died in the name of Patriotism.

And as always when the television coverage had ended there had been a curious mental echo. For what? The question had remained unasked . . . as it had always remained unasked. But it had been no less real. No less achingly sad. No less of a question because it had remained unasked and unanswered.

Eddie had muttered, 'Some "Brave New World",' and had shrugged a mac across his shoulders then left . . . presumably for the stage of *The Venus Fly-Trap* and the normal, half-hearted Sunday-afternoon rehearsal.

Freda was busying herself about the house. Moving around. Unable to relax sufficiently in order to remain still; performing unnecessary chores. Silent, set-faced. Living with her guilt. Living with her heartbreak.

Sidney Palmer pushed himself from the armchair and said, 'I'm going out, pet.'

'What?' Freda seemed to step from past misery to present concern.

'Out,' repeated Palmer. 'I'm going out for a walk.'

'The weather isn't fit . . .'

'It's November weather. People don't hibernate.'

159

'Sidney, I don't think you should . . .'

'Pet. I'm not going to hide here like a trapped animal. I've done nothing. Nothing! That means I can walk the streets.'

'Please!' It was almost a prayer. 'Be careful . . . for my sake.'

'That's what they want.' Gentle determination was in the tone. His eyes reflected understanding of his wife's wretchedness. The slight thrust of his chin gave hint of his resolution. He said, 'Fear. For people – decent people – to be afraid. That's what they want. All right! I'm calling their bluff. I'm going out. I'm walking where I want to walk. And they're not going to stop me.'

3.40 p.m.

Somewhere along the way – somewhere in Commercial Street – Palmer became aware of their presence. Like the 'feel' of a stare directed on to the back of the neck . . . that was his first inkling. He looked behind him and saw the car. The large Peugeot and its occupants, four broad-shouldered, hard-eyed men. 'Muscle'. 'Frighteners'. The car cruised alongside the kerb. At walking-speed, *his* walking-speed.

He muttered, 'You bastards!' and fought back the rising fear.

He varied his pace; sometimes hurrying, sometimes dawdling. The Peugeot varied its pace accordingly. A ploy. To ensure *he* was sure. There was no finesse – no subtlety . . . blatant intimidation.

He turned right. The car turned right after him.

Suddenly, as if on an impulse, he turned into Liverpool Street Station.

4 p.m.

They would, of course, expect him to catch the Tube. The classic way of shaking off a tail. Time would be lost while

160

they sent a man into the station, therefore make use of that time.

That had been his thought process.

He'd dodged behind a heap of parcels and Post Office bags. He'd waited, not even chancing a quick glimpse, in case his pursuers happened to be looking in that direction. He'd allowed time for the man – whoever the man was – to reach the Underground platform. To search, but not time enough to be certain and return to the main-line station. Then he'd left the station, paused at the entrance and looked for the Peugeot.

The Peugeot wasn't in sight.

He walked down Bishopsgate, past Wormwood Street, then turned right along Threadneedle Street. As he passed the junction with Old Broad Street, the Peugeot nosed its way out of the junction and resumed its position.

This time he walked at a steady pace. There was no need to vary his stride. He *knew*. But he also knew that within The City – if he kept to the major thoroughfares – he was safe.

The walking-pace 'chase' continued towards the river along Queen Victoria Street.

Somewhere – possibly at the junction with Cannon Street – the Humber joined the Peugeot. Some form of radio contact between the two cars . . . that was obvious.

The cat-and-mouse game continued at its funereal pace.

4.20 p.m.

He could have caught a Tube at Blackfriars.

He didn't. It was now becoming a matter of personal pride. This was why he was out. This was what he'd meant by 'walking where he wanted to walk'. Blast them to hell . . . he *wouldn't* be driven back to his home, as if it was the only place on God's earth left for him.

He swung left, then right at the Blackfriars complex, then

continued walking along the Victoria Embankment. Alongside the river. On *their* side of the road . . . a puny gesture of defiance.

He stopped alongside the moored H.M.S. *Discovery.* Stopped, faced the road, and waited. The two cars drew to a smooth halt alongside the kerb; the Peugeot in front of the Humber.

The front passenger-seat window of the Peugeot was wound down and Rhodes smiled across at Palmer. Palmer walked across to the car.

Rhodes said, 'We could give you a lift, of course.'

'No.'

'Home, perhaps?'

'I'm not going home yet.'

Rhodes shrugged.

Palmer said, 'Why?'

'Why?' Rhodes pretended not to understand.

'Did Hodge pass the message?'

'Some message,' said Rhodes off-handedly. 'Something about Peters.'

'He tried to kill me.'

'Did he?'

Palmer glanced at the Humber. Peters was behind the wheel.

'There.' Palmer jerked his head.

'What?'

'He's in the other car.'

'Maybe it's *him* you should be talking to.'

'I'll not beg,' said Palmer softly.

Rhodes said, 'No. It wouldn't do much good.'

'If . . .' Palmer paused, then said, 'If I gave you my word?'

'About what?'

'Do I have to tell you?'

Once more Rhodes shrugged.

'You'd be safe,' said Palmer.

'*I'm* safe,' smiled Rhodes.

They stared at each other for a moment.

Then Rhodes glanced up at the rain-heavy sky and mur-

162

mured, 'Keep walking, Palmer. We're all curious,' then wound up the window.

Palmer turned up his collar against the steady drizzle, turned from the car and continued along the Victoria Embankment.

4.40 p.m.

Again he could (perhaps) have lost them. He could have crossed the road, ducked into Embankment Station, used the Tube as a means of evading them: the Northern Line, the Circle Line, the District Line . . . those and others. So many levels. So many platforms.

The hell! Why should he? The object of the exercise . . . *not* to run. To show them that they were *not* Gods of the Earth.

Instead he turned left, crossed the river via the Hungerford Foot Bridge, reached the Concert Hall Approach, then zig-zagged among the cross-overs and cross-unders of the Royal Festival Hall and the Queen Elizabeth Hall network.

Why? He knew he couldn't guarantee to shake them from his trail, this way; two cars; one to do a U-turn and cross the river via Waterloo Bridge, the other to speed along the Victoria Embankment and cross on Westminster Bridge, then turn left along York Road. The perfect pincer movement.

So . . . why?

To taunt them, perhaps. To give Rhodes (and Peters) a 'sporting chance'. A deliberate flirting with danger. A gesture of defiance.

Something like that.

But also . . . Also (the truth, for God's sake!) also Freda.

She was the killer and, having killed, she'd stood aside and watched *him* put his freedom in jeopardy. All right . . . he'd *asked* her to. In the passage when he'd seen her and Mrs Hodge through the part-open door of the Ladies' toilets. When he'd *known*. He'd motioned them to keep out of sight – to keep quiet, he'd sent urgent messages with his eyes. Fine, she'd done only what he'd asked her to do.

But that she *had*!

Nothing to do with marriage. Nothing to do with a man's love for his wife or a woman's love for her husband. That, strangely enough, was still there. He thought no less of her.

But, y'know, self-preservation. That lingering doubt. That nagging 'perhaps'. Everything else he could handle. Everything else he could push aside and forget.

But not, y'know, the 'self-preservation' question mark.

Which for some crazy reason was why he was giving Rhodes and his heavies this even break. Because it didn't matter. Because *nothing* mattered whilever that 'self-preservation' thing haunted the back of his mind.

4.55 p.m.

They came at him from left and from right. On one of the high fly-overs. Deserted because of the time of day, because of the weather. because it was Remembrance Sunday. Not a soul in sight. Not a soul within earshot. The combination of so many things. So many little things.

Palmer sighed, leaned against the parapet and waited.

The two cars had been parked. The occupants – Rhodes, Peters and half a dozen hard-muscled bully-boys approached at a steady walking pace. Four from the right, four from the left.

Rhodes slipped a hand into the pocket of his jacket and the blade of the switch-knife shot from its housing.

The eight men arrived together.

Rhodes murmured, 'Foolish man,' and without pausing in his stride drove the blade hilt-deep into Palmer's rib-cage. As he struck he said, 'Peters.'

Peters moved his head in answer to his name. One of the heavies smashed a blackjack across the base of Peters's skull then caught him as he crumpled. A second heavy held Palmer upright.

Rhodes flipped a clean and folded handkerchief from his pocket. He withdrew the blade, wiped the handle of the

164

switch-knife then, holding the blade with the handkerchief, curled Peter's hand around the knife's haft.

He murmured, 'Okay. Move!'

Palmer's body was heaved over the parapet first. Then Peters's body . . . the right hand still held tight around the handle of the switch-knife. They tumbled and ended spread-eagled together on the road beneath.

Rhodes looked down at them for a moment. There was no expression on his face, no expression in his voice, as he spoke.

He drawled, 'That's awful. Two guys. So much hatred . . . eh? One shivs the other, the other pulls him over the top as he goes. That's bad. It shouldn't be allowed. I think somebody should notify the Law.'

Without fuss – without haste – the mobsters returned to their cars and drove away from the scene.

Thursday, November 16th

They drove from the crematorium in the V.W. Beetle. Just the two of them: Eddie and his mother. The battered old car somehow didn't seem out of place . . . as if it, too, was mourning and had aged and lost some of its energy within the last few days.

Just the two of them; Eddie and his mother.

In a dull voice and without taking his eyes from the road, Eddie said, 'I'm moving out, ma.'

'Y'mean . . .' She didn't end the sentence. There was no need to end the sentence. The communication between them – the mother-and-son bond – seemed not to require more than the bare minimum of words.

'I'm tired of mortuary visits, ma. Tired of inquests. Tired of watching coffins slide through curtains.'

'Tired of me?'

There was a childlike desire to be relieved of responsibility in the question. A plea for sympathy and forgiveness.

Eddie didn't answer . . . and that was answer enough.

She said, 'Where will you live?'

'Paul has a place.'

'Where?'

'Pimlico way. There's a spare room.'

'You've asked? Already?'

This time there was petulance. Self-pity, perhaps. The holding out of a hand by a woman drowning in her own sorrow.

'I'm moving out today,' grunted Eddie.

'Why?'

'Oh, ma . . .' It was a sigh and also a complete answer.

Eddie drove carefully. Slowly. As if each turn of the wheels was a carefully thought out progression along a route already decided upon.

166

She said, 'What about me?'

'You have friends.'

Softly she said, 'I have a son.'

'You had a husband.' The reply came back with the speed of a golf ball hurled at a wall. Its sheer velocity spoke volumes.

'Eddie!' she whispered.

'Sorry.' He shook his head. 'That was a lousy thing to say.'

She smiled for a moment. A smile of self-mortification. A resigned smile.

There was a silence.

She turned her head to look out of the side window as she murmured, 'It wouldn't cost you anything. What you pay now . . . it wouldn't even cost you that.'

'Ma,' he breathed. 'Don't . . . please.'

'I know. It's not for sale.'

Quietly – gently – he said, 'It never was.'

Monday, December 11th

It hadn't worked. The truth was it hadn't had a hope in hell of working. Paul was a nice guy, a good pianist and a fine jazzman, the one member of *The Opus* who might have made it work. Damn it . . . he'd *tried* to make it work. Come to that, so had Eddie.

But what had seemed minor differences while they'd shared the stand had become major differences when they shared more than the stand. When they shared the same kitchen. The same living room. The same bathroom. The same life.

No way!

Paul liked curry. A small thing, except that Paul also liked messing about in the kitchen *making* the curried meals. The damn place reeked of curry. Indian restaurants weren't in it.

And Eddie had thought he could live with some nice guy who liked spiced food, but no way! To crawl from bed, go to the kitchen in order to prepare something simple – toast and marmalade or scrambled eggs – and to be met by the overnight stench of curry. Jesus Christ, it was a little like breakfasting in a sewer.

Even music. Jazz was their bond. Correction . . . jazz *should* have been their bond. No way! Eddie's jazz was basic, small-combo, traditional stuff. But away from *The Venus Fly-Trap* – away from *The Opus* – Paul's taste was strictly 'progressive'. Clever-clever stuff. Technically out of this world. Musically (as far as Eddie was concerned) flash garbage without chord sequence, without melody line . . . without *anything*. And Paul had shelves of the damn stuff and a music centre which didn't seem to have a volume control capable of easing things down to even a moderate level.

That had sparked off their first row.

'For Christ's sake! Where does that crowd think it's heading?'

168

'That's clever, Eddie.'

'Clever?'

'That trumpet man. He's clever.'

'You call that high-register farting clever?'

'Hey, man. You blow a neat horn. But this stuff? No way.'

'The hell. I wouldn't *want* to.'

'Assuming you *could*.'

'Paul, I'm telling you, that crap is crap.'

'You *know*, eh?'

'Yeah. I know. Listen to the back-up. They don't know where the hell he is. Where the hell he's going next. Chances are *he* doesn't know.'

'Eddie, you should know. These cats don't fence themselves in with eight-bar, stone age stuff.'

'Yeah? *You* should know. "Cats" is the word. "Con" is the word. And *you*? That *you* should buy the con that that stuff's jazz.'

The first row. Okay, the first row, but it had left a bad taste. Two professional jazzmen and they couldn't even agree about their own music. What else could work?

Could be Eddie had imagined things, but he thought maybe Paul played even more 'progressive' garbage – and louder – after that first difference of opinion. If so, what could he do? It was Paul's pad . . . he could play *Land of Hope and Glory* backwards on a nose-flute and Eddie had no kick.

So there was bickering.

Too much hot water used for a bath. Some high-voiced chick Paul brought home as a one-night bed-warmer. Empty beer cans left littering the carpet. A lot of little things and they grew bigger as each man lost his sense of proportion.

Twice Eddie almost set off for Poplar. Both times the churned up bile deep in his guts dropped the anchor and held him back. Both times he walked the streets, searching for some solution, sniffing around in his mind for the right scent, but never finding it.

Then on the second Monday in December he reached a decision.

*

169

Tommy Hodge said, 'What's up north you can't get here?'

'Nothing. Maybe nothing.' Eddie held the trumpet at waist-height and fiddled with the valves.

'Then why the hell go?'

'Things,' said Eddie vaguely.

'I know, Eddie.' Hodge rested his hand on Eddie's shoulder. Like a father imparting wisdom to a son. He said, 'I know how it is. I know how you must feel.'

'The hell you do.' Eddie smiled.

'Your father . . . that's part of it.'

'Part of it,' agreed Eddie.

'He was a brave man, Eddie.'

'He was a bloody mug.'

'He took Peters with him. That can't have been easy.'

'From the start . . . he was a mug,' insisted Eddie.

'Your mother . . .' began Hodge.

Eddie cut him short and said, 'I don't want to hear.'

'I don't think you did the right thing. Moving in with Paul.'

'It wasn't the right thing,' agreed Eddie.

'So, go back to your mother and think about it.'

'I'm leaving,' said Eddie flatly.

'Does she know?'

'Ma?'

'Yeah, have you told her yet?'

'No.'

'Tell her, Eddie. She'll . . .'

'I know.' Eddie sighed. 'She'll pull out all the stops. Try to make me change my mind.'

'It mightn't be a bad thing.'

'I wouldn't know . . . and I don't give a damn.'

'Well, it's your life.'

'Yeah.' Eddie nodded.

Hodge seemed about to say something. Instead he closed his mouth, then said, 'The Christmas–New Year period? You'll stay till that's over.'

Eddie hesitated then said, 'Yeah, I guess.'

'Eddie . . .' Hodge looked worried.

170

'I'll stay,' insisted Eddie. He added, 'I *need* to stay.'

'Eh?'

'To – er – to find some other horn man to front *The Opus*.'

'Oh! Yeah.' Hodge seemed satisfied. 'Do that, kid.'

'The tables.' The impression was that Eddie was keeping his talk in line with his thought-process. 'New Year's Eve?'

'Uhuh?' Hodge looked puzzled.

'Are we booked solid?'

'Just about.'

'One table,' said Eddie. 'Can you fix it? For friends?'

'I guess.'

'As a favour?' said Eddie.

'Sure.' Hodge nodded. 'On the house, kid. We owe you.'

'Thanks.' Eddie smiled.

'How many?'

'Oh. I dunno.' Eddie seemed to make mental calculations. 'Say four. No more than four.'

'Great.' Hodge beamed his big-heartedness. 'Take it as a going-away present.'

'Thanks.' Eddie seemed satisfied. 'Thanks a lot.'

Tuesday, December 19th

And having made a decision – something of a snap decision – what then? So easy. In the make-believe atmosphere of *The Venus Fly-Trap* so obvious. But outside in the real world? With people . . . *real* people? That was when the balance had shifted a little.

He'd moved out of Paul's place; moved into one of the bed-and-breakfast dumps off Goodge Street. Somewhere to sleep for the few nights left of the old year. Not too expensive, not cheap for a room little larger than a telephone kiosk and a breakfast he rarely touched. But, y'know, not *too* expensive. This being London. This being the Christmas–New Year run-up. Itinerant musicians were supposed to live rough. Sleep in flea-pits. Substitute booze for food. All the books – all the movies – said so.

Okay. Come the New Year he was going to be an itinerant musician. That being so . . .

Sure, but the other thing? Not easy. A decision, but a decision very hard to transform into a fact. People were going to get hurt. People he'd once liked – once loved . . . people he didn't really *want* to hurt. People . . .

But on the other hand – and those same people – Jesus Christ, they could have done something. *Something*!

Thus he'd fumbled and stuttered a little.

'The – er – the Flying Squad, I suppose. The Murder Squad, perhaps?'

'And your business?' asked the receptionist.

'Oh, no! Not to you.'

'I'm afraid . . .'

'Look, miss . . . I'm sorry. Just the once telling. See? I'll tell it once. No more. It's about – about the shooting – the murder at *The Venus Fly-Trap*. About that. From that.'

172

The receptionist said, 'I'll see whether I can contact a plain clothes officer.'

'Not just anybody,' warned Eddie. 'Somebody I can talk to. Somebody who can *do* things.'

'I'll see what I can do.'

Thirty minutes later he was in a moderately comfortable office talking to a surprisingly young, surprisingly well-mannered detective inspector.

The D.I. listened to his story, then listened to his proposal.

Then the D.I. said, 'No immunity. We don't make deals. You understand that?'

Eddie nodded.

'And what.' asked the D.I., 'if we don't wait?'

Eddie said, 'Then you only get half the cake. The unimportant half.'

'You'd be surprised.' The D.I. smiled good-naturedly. 'Half a cake. We can start asking questions and, figuratively speaking, pop it back into the oven. We're very good cooks. We might end up with the full meal.'

'You might,' conceded Eddie. 'On the other hand, you might *not*. So, let's say I'm offering you the Lord Mayor's banquet.'

'That would be nice.' The D.I. nodded. 'Okay. Let's say we accept. I'll need to clear it, obviously. But I think the people carrying the necessary authority won't object. Do we need to see you again?'

'No. You know what *I'll* be doing. Be in the right place at the right time. What happens after that . . . that's your bag.'

The rough part. The part that damn near choked him. But having started, he couldn't stop. He couldn't stop, but to continue damn near choked him.

And yet his feelings hadn't to show. That too took some doing. To hide his heartbreak. To build a wall around his self-contempt . . . and the other thing.

It took less than half an hour. The longest half-hour – the most miserable half-hour – of his life.

And why?

Because she looked so lonely and defenceless. Just about the most pitiful person on God's earth.

'Come home, Eddie.' she pleaded.

'No way, ma. I cut the strings when pop died.'

'I – I can't sleep.'

'You seen a doctor?'

'What can *he* do?'

'Pills. Sleeping tablets . . . they can help.'

'Not for me, Eddie. I swear . . . not for me.'

'Okay, ma.' He took a deep breath. Let out a long sigh; a sigh of near-resignation. He said, 'Give me time to think on it.'

'No strings,' she promised.

'There never were any strings,' he grinned.

'You're my son. There's only you left.'

'Okay. Okay.' He raised a hand in a tiny gesture of re-straint. 'The rat-hole I'm living in now. Believe me that's a bigger argument than you could ever put up.'

'Then you'll . . .'

'I'll think about it, ma. Word of honour.'

'When?' she breathed.

'Soon. Within the next few weeks.'

'As long as that?'

'Ma, it's a decision *I* have to make. This last one – to leave home – okay it hasn't worked out. Not quite. But I need time.'

'But, Eddie . . . *weeks*.'

'I don't want to be wrong a second time, ma.'

'Eddie, I've nobody. Since your father . . .'

'I know, ma. And believe me, I don't want to hurt you. The last thing I want to do is . . .'

'Come home, Eddie. Please!' For a moment it seemed as if she might kneel at his feet.

He placed his arms around her shoulders and said, 'Okay, ma. We'll make a deal. We'll start a new year.'

'Wh-what?'

'Come to *The Fly-Trap*. I'll fix things with Valda. You can . . .'

'Eddie, I don't want to go to that place again. I don't want to go *near* . . .'

'It's okay, ma,' he soothed. 'I've fixed a table. A few friends. New Year's Eve. Valda . . . she'll be there. She'll look after you.'

'But look. I haven't any . . .'

'Get a nice outfit.' He slipped a billfold from his hip pocket. Peeled off a small wad of banknotes. 'Here. Take it. Get something nice. I'll tell Valda you're coming. She'll meet you. Then – before the night's out . . . you'll know.'

'Eddie, I can't . . .'

'Yes, ma. You *can*. It's what you need.'

'If – if . . .'

'That small thing. A gesture, eh? That the bad patch is over?'

And after that it was just a matter of pushing, gently in the right direction. Holding out a half-promise. Working on her undoubted misery. Nothing to it really. Like a kid greedy for candy . . . all she needed was steering in the right direction.

Handling things from the other end was comparatively easy.

Christmas Eve, Christmas Day, Boxing Day . . . they'd gone and *The Venus Fly-Trap* seemed to be gulping breath prior to that last, energy-sapping lap of New Year's Eve.

Valda took the groundbait without even being aware of the fact. There was the usual spell of relaxation – the normal late-afternoon sipping of booze prior to the wind-up before getting ready for the evening's miniature *mardi gras* – and Valda joined him at one end of the bar and, although she didn't know it, she came in there with her mouth wide open and greedy.

She said, 'You still leaving us, Eddie?'

'I guess.' He nodded.

'Your decision.'

'Sure.'

'We'll be sorry to lose you, kid.'

'You'll get along.'

She motioned for a drink. then said, 'Any particular reason? Or should I mind my own business?'

'Things,' smiled Eddie.

'Just things?'

'Worrying things.'

'You've had a rough year, Eddie.' She took her drink from the barman, sipped, then added, 'Things couldn't get worse.'

'Except . . .' He moved his shoulders.

'Yeah?' She looked interested. Concerned.

'Pop.' He paused, screwed his eyes in an effort of concentration. 'Okay, he was knifed. But Peters?'

'You think *not* Peters?' Genuine surprise was in her voice.

'A hunch. No . . .' He shook his head. 'More than a hunch. Something. Don't ask me what. Something I should know. Something I should remember. And when I do . . .'

176

'Then what?' she asked, gently.

'Maybe the fuzz. Maybe not. Either way, y'know, the big place isn't healthy any more.'

'So, you make for the sticks?'

He grinned and said, 'Village bobbies. They don't put two and two and make twenty-two.'

'Could be imagination,' she suggested.

'No.' He shook his head. 'It's up there somewhere. One day it'll surface.'

'You're that sure?'

'Yeah, I'm that sure.'

'Don't "honey-it's-okay" me.' Valda bit into the turkey sandwich – part of the left-overs from the Christmas beano – then, chewing, she added, 'If that kid's right. If there *is* something smelly about the way his old man got his. That just might leave me holding a very messy baby.'

'For Christ's sake! Peters knifed him, period.'

'Okay.' Still chewing Valda snapped, 'Why?'

Tommy Hodge leaned across, helped himself to a sandwich from the plate, and said, 'With Peters, why anything? His brains were puddled.'

'He was Rhodes's side-kick.'

'So?' Hodge bit into the sandwich.

'Tommy.' There was weary exasperation in her voice. She kicked off her shoes, leaned back into the cushions of the armchair, then said, 'The big man . . . Rhodes wanted him out of the way. Rhodes was – still is – a *very* ambitious man. Okay, we fed the big man to Eddie's mother and she jumped through the hoop. She thought she was saving Eddie from his own stupidity. That isn't important. Just that she pulled the trigger and killed the bastard Rhodes wanted her to kill. *And I helped.*

'Sidney went for a piss at a very awkward moment. That screwed things up beautifully. He saw me, he saw his wife . . . and he guessed. He kept his mouth zipped and he got away with it. But – like he says – the louts on the street don't read it that way. As far as they're concerned, Sidney Palmer was a very hot potato. Like Rhodes says. The simple arithmetic of the animals made Sidney Palmer bigger than the man he was supposed to have dropped. You with me so far?'

Hodge grunted an affirmative.

She continued, 'Rhodes . . . not Peters. Peters was a nothing. *Always* a nothing. The aggro between Peters and Eddie

178

wasn't important enough to count, except to Eddie's mother. But to Rhodes? That was a very different skittle-alley. He's top dog, but doesn't know it. Doesn't want to know it. Doesn't even want to be. But what *he* wants isn't important. The minds of the mobs run along their own twisted lines. Sidney Palmer, big kick any time he feels like taking up the option. Peters, second down the line after Rhodes. So, Rhodes blocks Palmer from every direction he's able. He even tries to fix him with a "road accident", but Peters makes a complete balls of it. Which means Rhodes decides to fix things personally.

'Palmer gets shivved and Peters ends up looking like *he* did it. But – question – why the hell *should* he? Unless, of course, orders from Rhodes. Me? I don't buy that. A man makes an arse-up of a hit-and-run routine . . . Rhodes is not likely to send him out with a knife to do something he couldn't do with a bloody motor car.'

'So you think Rhodes?' Hodge stretched his arms wearily.

'I think it's a possibility. I also think he's cocked that up, too.'

'Yeah?'

'Something.' She frowned. 'God knows what, but I think Eddie's spotted it.'

'You think that?'

'You interested?' she snapped.

'Rhodes is no mug.'

She glared and said, 'Rhodes is like everybody else. He's not perfect. He *can* make mistakes.'

'What mistakes?'

'Christ knows. But, if he *has*, that leaves your little honey-bunch half-way down the john and ready for somebody to press the flush lever.' She exploded, 'And don't you damn-well *care*?'

'Sure, I care,' he soothed. 'But, y'know you're tired. We need bed.'

'If I'm right,' she rasped, 'I'll have all the time in the world for bed. I'll have years in which to get rested up.'

'If you're right.'

179

'Look, pinhead, something's cooking. I can feel it. Eddie's booked a table. He's fixed it for Freda to whoop things up on New Year's Eve. He's asked me to look after her. Now that's something new. All these years . . . this is the first time he's done *that*.'

'So?'

'Some sort of Agatha Christie, last-page, this-is-how-it-happened set up.'

'You're out of your mind, honey.'

'And if I'm not?'

'Okay. Okay.' He swallowed the last of his sandwich. 'I'll pass it on to Rhodes. He'll figure something.' He rose from the chair. 'Now, for Christ's sake, cork it. Let's hit the sheets.'

Monday, January 1st

The New Year floated in on booze. It arrived with streamers and balloons; with tinsel and novelty hats; with all the noisy, roaring stupidity with which it always arrives. At *The Venus Fly-Trap* it had leaped on stage at the last stroke of midnight with an explosion of festival rowdyism which had not yet quietened . . . which would not quieten until long after the usual closing time.

The carpet of the dining-cum-concert-room was littered with coloured paper and cotton-wool snowballs. Every table was still occupied; would remain occupied until the drunks and the happy girls remembered they had a bed to go to . . . very often the same bed.

Not everybody was drunk. Not quite everybody. At a corner table Valda and Freda – and Eddie's two friends – weren't drunk. Relaxed, perhaps. Valda and Freda more than the two men; Valda and Freda had been drinking . . . just a little. Just enough to make them that little more buddy-buddy than might have been expected.

At Table Twenty-Seven Rhodes wasn't drunk. His companions were. Noisy drunk. Stupid drunk. But not Rhodes. With Rhodes the impression was that *he* decided; that given a whole bonded warehouse and, having poured every last drop down his throat, *he* would decide whether to be drunk or not.

But these were exceptions. The bulk of the customers were Happy-New-Year-ing in the established way. By shouting, cheering, dancing . . . getting friendly, and maybe too friendly, with every stranger within shouting distance.

On stage Eddie and *The Opus* closed the show. *Opus One* ended, Eddie bawled the usual good-night-and-thank-you spiel and the curtains closed.

Rhodes pushed himself from the table, and threaded his

181

way towards the side-stage door. The two men with Freda and Valda exchanged glances, then they politely excused themselves.

2.03 a.m.

Eddie Palmer walked down the passage leading from the stage to the dressing rooms. In the background – from the dining-cum-concert-room – the New Year's Eve whoopee formed a rising and falling of noise; for the umpteenth time the drunken, roaring chorus of *Auld Lang Syne* pushed its way through the separating doors and walls.

Eddie had left *The Opus* on stage, packing away their respective instruments, shuffling the various music scores back into their places in folders.

He walked down the passage. He pulled the mouthpiece from his trumpet, carried the mouthpiece in his right hand and the trumpet in his left. The fingers of his left hand fiddled with the trumpet's valves . . . the only outward sign of the disquiet which sickened his mind.

This was it. This *had* to be it. Right or wrong it was too late to turn back. This was definitely *it*.

2.05 a.m.

Eddie closed the door of the dressing room behind him. He leaned against the make-up shelf and blew the residue of spittle from the trumpet. He looked up as the dressing-room door opened then closed. As Rhodes entered. Eddie continued to 'dry out' his trumpet as Rhodes turned the key in the lock.

Somebody had to say something. Somebody had to make that first move. Open the conversation and, in so doing, concede some small victory to the other. Eddie shook the last of the spittle from the trumpet, turned and placed it carefully into its velvet-lined case. He closed the lid of the case. Rhodes might not have been there for what notice Eddie took of him.

Rhodes murmured, 'They tell me you're leaving. kid.'

182

'Yeah.'

Eddie picked an opened packet of cigarettes from the make-up shelf. He offered the open packet to Rhodes and Rhodes took a cigarette, then flicked a lighter and lighted first Eddie's cigarette then his own.

Rhodes said, 'It won't be the same without you, kid.'

'Horn men are easy to come by.'

'Good ones?'

'They're around.'

For a few moments they smoked in silence. Eddie unclipped his bow-tie and dropped it on to the seat of a chair.

'You have,' drawled Rhodes, 'had a rough year.'

'I've had better,' agreed Eddie.

'Your kid sister. Your old man. That's rough going, kid.'

Eddie grunted.

Rhodes said, 'Tommy thinks that's why.'

'He could be right,' said Eddie.

'They'll still be dead,' observed Rhodes. 'Here. Timbuktu. They'll still be dead.'

'Yeah.' Eddie drew on the cigarette then very deliberately said, 'Still have been murdered.'

'Your kid sister?' Rhodes raised quizzical eyebrows.

'As good as. Peters gave her the wherewithal.'

Eddie placed a foot on the seat of the chair and began to untie the lace of one of his shoes.

Rhodes said, 'Peters. You didn't like Peters?'

'He bounced me around. He killed my sister. No . . . I didn't dig him too deep.'

'He's dead.'

'Yeah.'

Eddie removed the shoe. Wriggled his stockinged toes, then placed the second shoe on the seat of the chair.

'Your old man killed him.'

Eddie concentrated his attention upon untying the second shoe-lace.

Rhodes said, 'Quite a guy, your old man.'

Eddie removed the shoe, wriggled his toes, then turned. He stood in his stockinged feet, with his hips against the make-up shelf, with his arms wide and resting on the edge of the shelf, with the cigarette held between the fingers of his right hand. Apparently at ease. Apparently unafraid.

He looked at Rhodes's face then very carefully, very slowly, said, 'Pa – my old man as you call him – never killed anybody in his whole life.'

2.08 a.m.

Like diving in at the deep end. Like that. You either swim or drown, so you'd better be able to swim. Eddie removed his right hand from the shelf and drew in a lungful of cigarette smoke. His eyes never left Rhodes's face. He looked so sure. So confident. But inside . . . he hoped to hell he *could* swim.

Very gently Rhodes said, 'That's not what the Law says, kid.'

'The Law,' said Eddie, 'figured he'd shot a bastard to death in the bog of this place. But we both know he didn't . . . don't we?'

'Do we?' teased Rhodes.

'Unless you have a very short memory. Unless you're dumb.'

'The gun came from you, kid.'

'Yeah, and to me from *you*.'

'No way.' Rhodes smiled.

'Or from somebody above you.'

'That I wouldn't know.'

'Okay.' Eddie drew on the cigarette again. 'Let's talk about what you *do* know. What we both know. The louse who was shot. He gave you orders.'

Rhodes pulled a face.

'Didn't he?' taunted Eddie.

'Everybody,' murmured Rhodes. He chuckled. 'The whole world, kid. Everybody giving orders. Everybody taking orders. Some people, like me, they don't *like* taking orders.'

'They like giving them?'

184

' "Yes",' admitted Rhodes, 'is a word I don't like using too often.'

'What I mean,' Eddie nodded.

'Just what *do* you mean, kid?'

'You and Valda . . . and somebody who stood in your way.'

'I walk over people who stand in my way,' said Rhodes quietly.

'No.' Eddie shook his head mockingly. 'You con them into a broom cupboard, then you get nice, middle-aged ladies to shoot them to death.'

2.10 a.m.

Eddie Palmer felt his stomach muscles knot up. There was more than one way of doing this thing. There was one right way . . . and a thousand wrong ways. He hoped this was the right way because, if it wasn't . . .

He watched Rhodes's face, saw the eyes narrow ever so slightly, saw the hint of tightness touch the lips.

Then Rhodes seemed to relax, smiled and said, 'You have guts, kid.'

'Not really. The truth doesn't scare me. that's all.'

'Your old lady could still be dropped. Ever thought about that?'

'Not without dropping Valda. And she'd drop you.'

'All worked out?' Rhodes held his head slightly to one side and smiled near-admiration. 'Like a row of dominoes.'

'A small push on the first,' agreed Eddie. 'They all fall.'

'So . . . don't push.'

'You scared of falling?' mocked Eddie.

'I'm scared of nobody, kid. Nobody and nothing.'

'Because Peters is out of the way?'

'Peters?' Rhodes made a spitting gesture.

'*He* should have been in that broom cupboard.'

'Peters wasn't worth a broom cupboard. He was a nothing.'

'So, why kill him?'

185

'Did I say?' Again the eyes narrowed and the tone hardened.

Eddie turned to squash out his cigarette in an ashtray on the make-up shelf. With his back to Rhodes, he allowed himself the luxury of a deep breath and a quick moistening of the lips.

As he turned to face Rhodes again, he said, 'Peters was killed . . . but not by my old man.'

'You say.'

'Pop wouldn't kill anybody. *Couldn't* kill anybody.'

'Everybody, kid. Nobody *can't* snap.'

'Where the hell did he get the switch-knife?'

'You crazy?' Rhodes stared.

'A head waiter. A very ordinary guy. Does *he* carry switch-blades around?'

'Peters did the knifing, goofhead. It was *his* knife.'

'*The hell it was!*'

Rhodes dropped what was left of his cigarette on to the floor, then slowly heeled it into shreds. He waited.

Eddie said, 'That knife. Not too fancy, but not common. Not the sort of cutlery for sale over a public counter. A nasty thing. A real killing tool.'

Rhodes still waited. His muscles seemed to have tensed as if ready for a spring. His eyes were cold and unblinking. He waited for what Eddie had to say next.

Eddie said, 'I saw that knife at the inquest . . . for the second time. The first time? July – about the middle of July – when *you* used it to back Peters down a hole.'

'You're very observant, kid.' The words were soft and threatening.

'All my life,' said Eddie. 'I can count on the fingers of one hand how many times I've seen a switch-blade. The last two times, the same one. Yours. Don't lie to me, Rhodes. A big man like you. A little guy like me. You don't have to lie to *me.* You shivved my old man, then you threw Peters over the edge as Patsy.'

'No.' The drawl returned and, with the drawl, the squat Browning .25 automatic which Rhodes slipped from his inside breast pocket. 'I don't have to lie to you, kid. You guess too good.'

'You gonna use that?' The question was a little breathless. The voice was a little harsh and dry.

'I'm not gonna pick my teeth with it.' Rhodes smiled.

'Okay.' Eddie held up a hand, as if to ward off the bullet. 'Before you pull the trigger . . . one question.'

Rhodes shrugged.

'Why pop? What the hell had *he* done to deserve the treatment?'

'He'd walked away from a murder charge.'

'He was innocent.'

'I know that, kid. You know it. But the boys on the street? They believe in fairies. A man stops a murder charge . . . he's a killer. He *has* to be, otherwise the cops wouldn't stand him in a dock. He walks away from that dock . . . that makes him big. Too big. Too big for me to let him walk loose.' The smile broadened into a grin. 'Stupid, eh? But, y'know, the boys on the street still think our policemen are wonderful.'

'They are,' gasped Eddie. 'Especially the two on the other side of that door who've been listening to this conversation.'

'Balls!'

Rhodes chuckled as he squeezed the trigger.

187

Tuesday, April 3rd

The detective inspector looked uncomfortable. Awkward and on edge. He tasted his coffee and watched Eddie Palmer across the table. Eddie was staring through the plate-glass; staring across the road, to where the broad, shallow steps led into the arcade-like entrance to the Central Criminal Court.

Remembering.

Remembering a Wednesday in November.

The D.I. cleared his throat and said, 'The leg. How's the leg?'

'Okay.' Eddie turned his head. His hand automatically touched the fleshy part of his right thigh. 'It's okay. More or less mended.'

'Two-fives. They're nasty, but rarely lethal.'

'Yeah.'

'Er – good job that door was flimsy. Just the one shot.'

'Yeah.'

Eddie glanced out of the window again at the shallow steps, at the gloomy entrance.

'How long?' he asked hoarsely.

'Life,' muttered the D.I.

'Oh for Christ's sake!'

'All right.' The D.I. sighed then, with some reluctance, said, 'A guess. that's all. Rhodes . . . about twenty. Maybe a little less, but I doubt it. We threw the book at him. So, I'd say twenty.'

'And ma?'

'Maybe ten.'

'Oh, Jesus!'

'Look, Eddie.' The D.I. kept his voce low. 'She committed murder, old son. Deliberately. She murdered the wrong guy, but the law isn't interested in that. Okay, she had an excuse – what *she* thought was an excuse – that might count in her

188

favour. Mrs Hodge *didn't* have that excuse. She knew damn well who was in that cupboard. *She'll* be lucky if she comes out with less than fifteen. Hodge? Well . . . accessory after. He'll do what the judge gave him. Five minus good behaviour. And you?' The D.I. smiled. 'Two years, suspended, for having the gun. The law works that way. It's a good law.'

'She won't make it,' groaned Eddie.

'Your mother?'

'She won't come out alive.'

'She's not old, Eddie. Not really *old*.'

'She killed pop. That's the way she'll look at it. For what she did pop died. *That's* what'll kill her.'

'I dunno.' The D.I. frowned. Then he said, 'Can I ask a question? Off the record?'

'Sure.'

'Why?' The voice of the D.I. was low, and sympathetic. '*You* put your mother inside. Why?'

Eddie hesitated, then said, 'Because she *did* kill pop. She committed murder, then stood aside and let pop suck the hammer. That. And, from that, he was knifed.' He paused, then continued, 'Two parents. You love 'em both. But one has the edge, always. With me it was pop. He worked in a dirty world, but kept himself clean. That's not easy. And for *that* . . .' Once more he paused, then whispered, 'I couldn't let it happen. The people who did *that* to him. Whoever they were . . .'

Eddie tried to explain, but knew he wasn't getting through. The love of a son for his mother; the big love, the great love, the legendary love. And – okay – it happened. A good son loved his mother. Loved her like crazy. But, just *sometimes*, he loved his father even more.

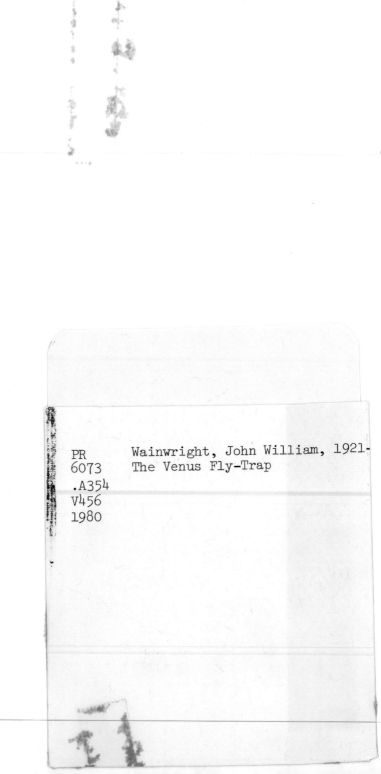